BELLES

A Carolina Love Story

Karen Stokes

GREEN ALTAR BOOKS
Columbia, South Carolina

BELLES, A CAROLINA LOVE STORY

Published by GREEN ALTAR BOOKS
An Imprint of Shotwell Publishing, LLC
P.O. Box 2592
Columbia, South Carolina 29202

www.shotwellpublishing.com

This is a work of fiction. Any similarity with real persons or events is purely coincidental. Persons, events, and locations are either the product of the author's imagination, or used fictitiously.

Cover image of Carl Sandburg National Historic Site in Flat Rock, North Carolina, used courtesy of National Park Service.

SECOND EDITION

ISBN-13: 978-1947660113
ISBN-10: 194766011X

PROLOGUE

Today I am thirty years old.

Harriott had not intended to write much more than this in her diary entry for June 9th, 1863, but after a thoughtful pause, she lifted her pen again and continued.

For a number of years, people have regarded me as an old maid, and now, on the thirtieth anniversary of my birth, I think I must finally accept the designation. Yet I do not feel old—quite the opposite in fact— nor do I feel any of the discontent or sourness of disposition that others often ascribe to spinsters like me. I am fortunate in many ways. My father has wealth, so I have not lacked for material things. I have a good family whom I love, many good friends, and useful occupations. Being unmarried, I have no children of my own, but I have helped to raise a few, and others that will come along, I expect. I could call my life nearly perfect…if not for this terrible war, which has changed everything for everyone. It has taken away some of those whom I loved, and may at any moment take more.

On this day, she had meant to express only thankfulness for her numerous blessings, but thinking, as she often did, of her brother, cousins and many friends in the army, all in constant danger, she added in a sudden outburst of anxiety, *Oh, Lord, who will be next? And when will all this senseless death and destruction end?*

CHAPTER ONE

Flat Rock, North Carolina, June 1863

Mrs. Stiles sat up in her bed in the darkness, terrified, and certain now that the strange noises she heard had come from *inside* the house.

Her heart was racing, but as her drowsiness wore off, she suddenly remembered that she had a guest, and that the noises might be her brother moving about in the bedroom just down the hall. Captain Mitchell had arrived that morning, to stay in his sister's home while he recuperated from an injured leg. Mrs. Stiles wondered if he had fallen or hurt himself somehow in the unfamiliar surroundings. She pulled on a robe, felt her way to the door, and stepped into the hall. At the threshold of her brother's bedroom she saw a light and, the next moment, the door opened. Captain Mitchell came out in a nightshirt. Seeing his sister, he put a finger to his mustache to signal silence as he quietly closed the door behind him.

His grim expression sent another wave of terror through her. Obviously he had heard the same noises, and thought there must be someone else in the house. He was gripping a pistol in one hand and with the other holding a cane, shifting the weight of his injured leg to it as he began to hobble down the stairs. Mrs. Stiles meanwhile occupied herself in urgent prayers for divine protection.

Captain Mitchell moved down the steps slowly and carefully, his way illuminated by the bright moonlight flooding in through a small octagonal window above the stairs. When he reached the first floor, he could see the front door shake, then begin to open. He took cover behind a tall cabinet near the stairway, but craned his neck out far enough to keep one eye fixed on the door. It soon opened wide enough to reveal the silhouette of a short, stocky figure in a greatcoat. The man was holding a rifle, and his figure bulged at the waist with what appeared to be several haversacks or pouches.

The captain drew back to fully conceal himself. The intruder moved toward the stairs, and as soon as he passed by the cabinet, Captain Mitchell moved forward and pressed a pistol to his back.

"Put down the rifle," he said.

Startled, the man lowered his firearm, but did not drop it.

"Who's that?" he gasped, adding quickly, "I—I am hunting deserters, and saw them come this way —"

"Put down the rifle," the captain repeated menacingly.

The man slowly leaned over to place the rifle against the wall, but as he raised himself up, he abruptly turned and tried to thrust away the pistol jammed against his ribs. The captain kept his hold on the pistol, but it was pushed aside, aimed only at the floor. The intruder took hold of his wrist, and a struggle began. Wrestling for control of the weapon, the two men reeled across the parlor, smashing into a side table and chair. The man in the greatcoat bellowed in pain as he lost his balance, fell back, and collided with the sharp corner of the table. He was stunned long enough for the captain to wrest himself from the strong grip of his right hand.

Grunting and panting, the intruder pulled out a large Bowie knife from a sheath buckled across his chest, but his lunge was checked by the firing of the pistol, and he fell backwards from the blast that ripped into his throat. Staggering, Captain Mitchell nearly toppled over on to the man, but caught himself on the overturned chair and held the gun on his attacker, uncertain at first where the bullet had hit him.

Though nearly faint with fear, his sister had made her way down the stairs with a candle.

"Jim! Jim! Are you all right?" she cried, trembling like a leaf.

"I'm all right," he answered breathlessly.

"What's happened?"

"Our housebreaker is dead, I think."

"Oh, thank God you were here!" she groaned. She felt weak, and leaned against the banister for support.

The captain went to a front window and peered outside. A lone, weary-looking horse was tethered to a fence post, but apart from that, no living thing in the form of man or beast was to be seen.

"Oh, Jim, take care!" cautioned his sister.

"Come, Sarah," he said reassuringly. "I think there is no danger now. I believe this man was alone. Light a lamp, please."

Sarah obeyed and lit an oil lamp, the glow of which clearly revealed the dead man's face—a rough, craggy, pock-marked face bristling with a wiry red beard. His stout body had slipped off the table to the floor, and dark red blood seeped into the carpet around his head. The contents of one of the haversacks draped over his shoulder had spilled out; it was full of dozens of pieces of paper which, upon closer inspection, turned out to be letters.

"He's robbed the mail!" Sarah exclaimed.

One of the letters was beginning to absorb a blood stain. She automatically snatched it away, but instantly dropped it in revulsion.

"Do you think he is one of the Tories?" she asked her brother.

"Most likely," said the captain, returning to her side.

"Tory" was the name given to unionists—North Carolinians who had remained loyal to the United States. The Tories who had armed themselves to operate as irregular combatants and enemies of the Confederates were called bushwhackers. Some were disaffected local men; others were deserters who had drifted into the region from other parts of the state or farther off, finding good hiding places and retreats in the mountains. While some wore Yankee uniforms, and may have been deserters from that army or in its pay, many were apparently deserters from the Southern army, or those resisting the Confederate draft, which was greatly resented by the independent mountaineers. The bushwhackers conducted guerilla warfare against the Confederacy, but a number of them were not so much soldiers as criminals who used the pretext of partisanship to commit thievery, and worse.

The flap of another haversack was open and in it a handsome gold watch and chain was partly visible. The captain picked up the timepiece and admired it in the lamplight.

"I wonder whose this was?" he mused.

"Perhaps we can return these things to their rightful owners," Sarah suggested.

"We can try."

"How dreadful, dreadful!" she whispered, still trembling as she gazed down at the dead man. "Oh, when I think that he might have killed you! Are you hurt, dear? Are you in pain?"

The captain's injured leg was aching sharply, but he kept this information to himself. Seeing how distraught his sister was, he put an arm around her thin shoulders to comfort her, studying her wan, troubled face with a surge of pity and protectiveness.

Mrs. Stiles had been living alone for months now. After staying with various relatives in upstate South Carolina to escape a feared invasion of Charleston, she had taken refuge in her family's Flat Rock summer home while her husband and two sons served in the Confederate Army. Their regiment had recently been sent to the neighboring state of Tennessee, and Sarah wanted to live as close to them as possible in order to be with them sooner and longer during their furloughs. As she waited for their return and the end of the war, day upon day, month upon month, and year upon year of constant anxiety for them had taken its toll on her and left physical marks. Her dark hair had become streaked with gray, and her face, always plain, was plainer now with its perpetually careworn look. At forty-two (seven years older than her brother) she looked more like a woman well into her fifties.

Sarah slipped an arm around the captain's waist, reassured by the strength she felt in his tall, powerful, well-formed frame, and he held her closely for a few moments. She looked up at him and remembered their father, James Mitchell the elder (dead for many years now, but still a vivid memory for her), thinking how much his son James was like him, sharing the same "Black Irish" looks—not exactly handsome, but strong and manly, with fair skin, dark hair, and blue-green eyes.

"I'm going to leave this man here for the night," he said. "I shall need some help to remove the body in the morning."

Brother and sister made their way back upstairs, and that night Sarah lay awake in her bed for a long while, unable to sleep until a few hours before sunrise.

* * *

The next morning dawned bright and cloudless, promising a

beautiful day. Sarah woke from her uneasy, shallow slumbers at the usual hour and rose to comb her hair, but she waited until she heard her brother stirring before she came out of her room, still clad in her nightgown and robe. James was fully dressed, wearing civilian clothes now rather than the gray uniform he had worn the day before.

After breakfast which, on that particular day, consisted only of some tea and milk, she was anxious to have the dead body removed from her house. Servants wrapped the corpse in part of the rug and placed it in a small wagon which Captain Mitchell drove into the nearby village of Hendersonville, the dead man's horse following along behind.

A few hours later, Sarah was full of questions when her brother returned alone. She met him in the carriage drive with two of her servants, Binah and July, a married couple, who were also very curious to know about the housebreaker. July, a thin, wiry black man of fifty, took the captain's cane and helped him down from the wagon.

"Well, you should have seen what came out of those haversacks," he said, shaking his head. "All kinds of things came out of them, as well as the dead man's pockets. The magistrate has them now, with the mail, and will post a notice so that people can come to identify their belongings. A lady in town claimed the horse, and said it had been stolen from her place last week."

"Who was he?" asked Sarah. "Did anyone know him?"

"Someone said that he was part of Jake Kendall's gang, and had worked alone before."

July gave a drawn-out whistle and remarked knowingly that Kendall was a "bad, bad man."

"How I wish the government would send some soldiers here to hunt down those ruffians! It isn't safe to live here anymore with such men about," Sarah complained. "Is there any word that we shall receive help?"

Her brother shook his head regretfully.

"There's no word on that," he said, "though the magistrate told me that the militia may be ordered out soon."

"It's the army that should be dealing with these men, not the militia. It's not right we should be threatened so!" she fretted.

By early afternoon, the captain and his sister had regained some of their appetite. After a light meal, Sarah went upstairs for a nap, and James sat down in the parlor to read a newspaper he had picked up in Hendersonville. In the room servants had already cleared away the blood soaked carpet, scrubbed the wooden floor beneath it, and covered part of the area with a smaller rug. While getting comfortable in the chair, he noticed a small piece of paper that had fallen into the space between the cushion and the arm. As he took hold of it and pulled it up the paper tore, one corner being held down by his weight. He moved his leg and lifted the paper out, still in one piece but damaged. Marked by a blood stain in one corner, it was the letter his sister had rescued the night before. The little envelope, now almost completely separated from the torn sheet inside, was addressed to a "Miss Mary McCord, Greenville, South Carolina" in a delicate, beautiful, feminine script.

The letter was now visible, and he could see the same handwriting on the part now exposed. He hesitated to peruse it any further, but thought he ought to at least determine the name of the sender. He took the sheet out of the dangling envelope and opened it. At the end of the letter he found the signature of "Harriott M."

Later, when his sister came down from her nap, James asked her if she knew of a lady in Flat Rock by that name.

"Harriott M.," she repeated thoughtfully, then quickly replied, "Oh, yes! That must be Miss Harriott Middleford. Why do you ask?"

He held up the damaged letter.

"I believe this belongs to her. I found it in the chair."

Sarah took the paper, her fingers avoiding the bloodied corner, and read the address.

"I don't know this Miss McCord," she said, "but I do know that the Middlefords have relations in Greenville, also refugees from Charleston, I think."

Middleford was a name well known in Charleston. They were one of the richest, most venerable families in the South Carolina lowcountry, having as their ancestors several distinguished patriots of the Revolution, including a signer of the Declaration of Independence. Some of the Middleford ladies had left the besieged city of Charleston to take refuge in Flat Rock, a place of summer retreat for many wealthy South Carolinians for some three decades. So many Charleston families owned residences here that this picturesque cluster of country estates in western North Carolina had come to be known as "The Little Charleston of the Mountains."

Sarah opened the letter, holding the two torn sections together.

"Sarah!" her brother reproved her. "We ought not to read that."

"I only wish to confirm that it is the Harriott M. I know, and not another," she said. "Oh yes, yes, it is she. She mentions her sisters by name, and writes of her thirtieth birthday this week."

He stared at his sister doubtfully as her eyes continued to pore over the letter.

"Listen to this, Jim," she said, ignoring his "tsk" of disapproval. "Today, my dear Mary, I am inclined to look over my life and contemplate its changes, and my present state. Imagine my feelings at the age of eighteen if I had been told then, that at the age of thirty, I should be an old maid, plain as a homespun dress, with reading and writing for my principal diversions. Yet I find that I am content, and perfectly satisfied with my lot in life, and desire nothing of Heaven but a change in some circumstances relating to those I love..."

"Sarah," he said again reprovingly, interrupting her. "Those words were not meant for our eyes."

His sister closed the letter and folded the pieces together.

"I only read a small portion," she sniffed. "Yes, I know I read a little more than necessary, but there is no reason for Miss Middleford to know that. I think I shall return it to her—it can't be sent off like this. Tomorrow I shall pay a call on the Middlefords. No, I shall invite them here after church Sunday. They will want to meet you."

"Must we have guests so soon?" he grumbled.

"Soon? Sunday is several days from now! Don't you wish to meet the people here? A gentleman of your age is a rare thing in these parts, you know, especially a single gentleman. You will be very popular."

"I'm not interested in popularity," said the captain. "I came here to convalesce."

"You will certainly be bored with only my company after a while," she predicted. "Then you will be glad for some other."

"Dear sister, you don't bore me," he assured her.

Sarah left him to see after some housework and the preparations for the evening meal, and he turned his attention back to his newspaper. After a few minutes he felt himself growing drowsy, and closed his eyes to nap a while in the chair, and soon, the words his sister had read from the letter replayed in his mind. For some reason, they vaguely intrigued him, and he wondered what this Miss "Harriott M." was like. She was interesting, he thought, this lady...but before ruminations could take him much further, the captain had fallen asleep.

CHAPTER TWO

Sunday came and brought with it the promise of visitors in the early afternoon. The dining table was set with edibles appropriate for a light luncheon, and Sarah and her maidservant, Binah, fussed over the final touches while Captain Mitchell enjoyed the intermittent sunshine from the front porch, or, as the Charlestonians called it, the piazza. He was hungry, and for purely selfish reasons, hoped the guests would arrive promptly.

The Stiles' residence was one of the smallest and oldest in Flat Rock. Mr. Stiles had purchased it just before the war with intentions to renovate and enlarge it, but all those plans had been postponed indefinitely when he and his sons enlisted in the army. Though the house was in need of some repair, it had very pleasant surroundings. From the piazza, the captain looked out on a beautiful expanse of green lawn shaded by hemlock, oak, and pine trees. The yard sloped down a hill to a lovely oval pond encircled by woods. Just above the trees that surrounded the water, the highest peaks of a faraway mountain range were visible on clear days. Today, the sky was clouded and a solid bluish gray in that direction, obscuring the line between sky and earth, so that no mountains were to be seen.

Sarah soon joined her brother on the piazza and took a chair next to his. After a nearly half an hour had passed, James began entertaining some ill-feelings towards the Middlefords. His sister saw him chewing at one corner of his dark mustache, a nervous habit of his that often indicated irritation.

"What time were you expecting these ladies?" he inquired, drumming his fingers on the arm of the chair.

"After the church services," she replied. "They ought to have been here by now, unless Reverend Reade's sermon was a lengthy one. They sometimes are, I'm afraid."

Though Mrs. Stiles was a Presbyterian, she often attended the Episcopal chapel in Flat Rock and was well acquainted with the elderly rector's habits.

"I suppose we must wait for them," the captain sighed, "and make ourselves martyrs to politeness."

Sarah laughed at her brother's nonsense. After waiting in silence another minute or two, they heard from a distance the sounds of female voices, and soon, a procession of five ladies came into view.

"The Middlefords," said Sarah.

The ladies were dressed as well and as fashionably as possible in a time when even ordinary fabrics and decent shoes were rarities (silks, ribbons, and other such fineries being almost unheard of). Most of the dresses they wore were made of homespun fabric, but they were neat and well-fitted, and enhanced with pretty sashes, laces, and other adornments taken from older, finer clothes now in tatters.

A gray-haired, matronly lady with a walking stick and an aristocratic bearing led the way, followed by three young women who were putting their heads together in eager conversation. Some distance behind these four sauntered a tall, slender woman holding a yellow parasol. Struck by her gracefulness and preoccupied, contemplative air, the captain turned to his sister to ask, "Who is that elegant lady? The one following the rest."

"*That*," Sarah replied, mirthfully compressing a big smile down to a little simper, "is Miss Harriott M."

As the five drew closer to the house, Captain Mitchell scanned all the female faces in the order in which they approached. The first, who was obviously the mother of the brood, looked as though she might have been a great beauty in her prime. There were three pretty faces behind her, one very girlish, the other two somewhat more mature. The face of Harriott M., who had now quickened her pace a little in order to catch up with the others, was handsome rather than pretty, long and somewhat sharply cut, but softened by calm gray eyes and a pleasant mouth. Her fine, silky, lustrous hair was a light brown color, so light a brown as to be almost blonde. The other young women were darker brunettes.

When the ladies reached the piazza, Sarah began to make the introductions, and her brother, who had worn his uniform today, bowed with a formal, military manner as he made the acquaintance of the family—Mrs. Middleford, Miss Harriott M., and her sisters Louisa, Rebecca, and Charlotte—or, as the siblings called each other, Harrie, Lou, Beck, and Lottie.

"You must forgive our lateness, Mrs. Stiles," said Mrs. Middleford. "We shall have to place the blame on Mr. Reade, who went on too long this morning."

"Much too long," groaned Charlotte, the youngest daughter, comically rolling her eyes.

Amused by the girl's performance, the captain nearly laughed aloud, but, noting the mother's frown of disapproval, he immediately checked himself.

All filed into the house, where, in the dining room, Sarah

received many compliments on her attractive table settings brightened with colorful wildflowers. Though ravenously hungry, her brother waited politely until all the ladies had served their plates, and then filled his own with a casual air, as if perfectly indifferent to the food. Fortunately for him, his sister was more interested in conversation than eating, and while she related some interesting news about a mutual friend, he was able to finish one modest helping and serve himself another.

Soon, however, the ladies turned all their attention to the newcomer, and eagerly asked him to tell them about his exciting and deadly encounter with the housebreaker. Before the captain could begin an answer, his sister enthusiastically launched into praises and descriptions of his fearlessness and daring that night, and he shifted uncomfortably in his chair while she effused, obviously embarrassed by her exaggerations.

"I had the advantage of surprise," he explained, when Mrs. Stiles paused a moment to catch her breath.

"Yes, but you were at a disadvantage because of your injuries," Sarah pointed out, though, after this remark, she relented and allowed her brother to tell the story and satisfy their guests' curiosity.

Miss Harriott winced when the captain described how his sister snatched away the letter that was soaking up drops of the dead man's blood, and Sarah shuddered at the memory of it. She had sent the letter over to Miss Middleford the day after the incident, and wondered aloud now if she had forwarded it on to Greenville.

"No," Harriott replied. "I destroyed it, and sent another in its place."

"I would have done the same," said Sarah. "I thought of destroying it myself, but decided I ought to leave that up to you, since it was your letter."

"I wouldn't have minded if you had destroyed it. It was of little consequence. I am so thankful, though, that your brother was there to protect you."

"Oh, it was providential," Sarah said feelingly, clasping her hands together. "Providential!"

Mrs. Middleford nodded in earnest and grave agreement, then, changing the subject, she inquired about the captain's injuries.

"Is it expected that you will fully recover the use of your limb?" she asked.

"I don't expect that it will ever be as good as it was," he replied, "but I hope it may improve in time."

Sarah informed the ladies that Captain Mitchell had made a wonderful recovery so far, and that she expected him to someday do quite well without the aid of a cane.

"After James was wounded in Virginia, our mother went to Richmond to nurse him," she went on. "He was not in a hospital, but in the private home of a gentleman who had taken him in. When she entered James's room, she found him in bed, lying with his wounded limb in a sling which was tied from a chandelier overhead! One of the doctors had recommended amputation, but my brother was determined to keep his body whole if possible, and found another physician who was willing to try to save the leg, though James was warned that his life was at risk."

"I thought I had as good a chance of surviving with the injured limb as without it," the captain put in, to explain his willingness to take that risk.

"Oh, the anxieties our poor mother suffered on his account!" Sarah sighed. "It took several months before he was able to walk again, on crutches of course, and, after Mother took him back to Camden with her, several weeks more before he could get about with a cane."

"Your mother took refuge in Camden?" asked Mrs. Middleford.

"Yes, when it became too dangerous in Charleston she rented a house on Hobkirk Hill," Sarah explained. "She has been comfortable there, and has relatives in town, but she thought it best that James spend the summer in a cooler, healthier place, and so sent him to me."

"I'm very grateful to be alive, and to be able to get about as well as I do," he concluded, hoping to close the subject.

"It was God's providence, yes, God's providence," Mrs. Middleton stated decisively, as if there could be no other view on the matter. Providence was on her mind a great deal that morning, having been the subject of Rev. Reade's lengthy sermon.

"I'm sure you are right, Mrs. Middleford," the captain responded graciously.

"You must come and visit our pretty chapel here in Flat Rock, Captain," Louisa suggested.

"I'd like that," he said.

"I don't know that you are up to such a walk yet, Jim," his sister admonished him. "The church is more than a mile from here."

"I could ride or drive there in the carriage," he reminded her. "But I've been taking some walks for the past few days, and I might try a longer one soon."

* * *

In the course of the next hour, the captain learned much about his sister's guests. Mrs. Middleford's husband, an elderly but still very fit and able man, had remained at one of his rice plantations in the Georgetown District of South Carolina, trying to keep it operational despite many difficulties. Mrs. Middleford, who always looked to her husband to make most decisions and regulate family affairs, seemed at something of a loss without him, but had so far managed to do at least tolerably well without his direction, often relying on the good sense and judgment of her eldest daughter, Harriott. In addition to her own daughters, Mrs. Middleford's household also included two orphaned grandsons, the children of another daughter who had died just before the war, and whose father had been killed in Virginia in one of the first battles.

The Middleford girls told the captain all about their spinning wheel and "weaving machine," as they called it, with which they manufactured their own cloth—homespun for themselves and their servants, and for friends and relations in the army. In the relative isolation of Flat Rock, it was one of the few ways they could contribute to the war effort.

Eventually, Captain Mitchell and the ladies went out to the piazza, but the sunshine had disappeared by this time. It had grown cloudy; strengthening breezes and a darkening sky boded an approaching storm. Mrs. Middleford regretfully announced that she and her daughters needed to leave now in order to get home before it began raining. She invited Mrs. Stiles and her brother to her home, extracting a promise from the captain that he would visit often.

When the Middleford ladies had departed and were out of sight, James returned to his chair on the piazza, and his sister sat down next to him with a contented expression.

"That went well," she said. "You see, I told you that you would be very popular. The ladies were well pleased with you, I could tell."

And while Sarah talked more with her brother about the day's guests, who were now making their way home, the Middleford sisters were walking together arm in arm behind their mother and airing their opinions about Captain Mitchell. Before his arrival, Mrs. Stiles had told them a few things about her brother, and they had been eager to meet this gentleman, not only because he was a Charlestonian, and a wounded officer of their army, but also because he was a single man—a widower of some five years.

Charlotte seemed a little displeased with the captain, thinking of how his dark, downturned mustache, and the deeply etched lines that led down to his lips, gave him a somewhat stern, frowning look.

"He has such a stern face," she said. "As though he disapproved of us all."

"Oh, you are too sensitive," Rebecca protested, and then teased her sister, "Perhaps he only disapproves of you."

Harriott interrupted the laughter that followed to remark, "The captain has a strong face, I should say, and it is true that the expression of his mouth lends a certain look of severity to it, but that is just an accident of nature, and I do not think it indicates his character. I found him quite amiable."

"He seems very intelligent and gentlemanly," Louisa agreed. "I like him."

"I wish he were a handsome man," sighed Charlotte.

"He's not so bad-looking," Rebecca countered. "But even if he were handsome, he is too old for you, and you are too silly for him."

This insult brought on a prolonged, shrill argument between the two youngest sisters, and to avoid it, the older sisters, Harriott and Louisa, separated from Charlotte and Rebecca and slowed their pace to put some distance between them.

"So you found Captain Mitchell amiable?" Louisa queried.

"Didn't you?" Harriott responded.

"Oh, yes! Mama liked him very much, too, I could tell. She will be wanting him as a guest just as often as possible, I'm sure. But poor Lottie, she is so disappointed."

Harriott shook her head.

"Most likely Lottie has been imagining him as a divinely handsome, romantic officer who would somehow, for some reason, fall in love with a sixteen year old girl."

"I'm sure it's plausible in her young mind," laughed Louisa.

Harriott studied her sister with evident amusement. Louisa asked her why she was smiling.

"All of you seem so young to me," she replied.

"I am twenty now!" Louisa protested mildly. "Nearly twenty-one!"

Harriott put an arm around her sister and admired her youthful, beautiful face, a slightly elongated oval of perfect complexion and coloring.

"Well," she said, "I suppose I must put you in a different category now, Lou. You are indeed a woman grown—but far from spinsterhood like me."

Louisa hesitated to answer, but then ventured delicately, "You—you need not have been so. Do you regret it, Harrie?"

"Why, no. But I should regret it for you, dear. I don't think it is your fate."

They walked on in silence for a while, until Harriott worked up the courage to ask Louisa if she had received another letter lately from their cousin Weston, a young man who had loved Louisa since childhood, and wanted to marry her. Louisa had refused his proposal of marriage just before the war.

"He wrote to me again last week," she answered curtly, frowning with irritation. "But he knows better than to speak of certain things to me."

And the look she gave Harriott was sufficient to bring that subject to a conclusion.

* * *

Later, at home, Charlotte sighed and stood at a parlor window watching a steady, soaking rain which had just begun. She was longing for solitude, but there was none to be had inside the house, and the weather prevented her from going outside.

Harriott was seated nearby reading a letter from a relative. Growing bored with the rain, Charlotte turned to her and asked if there was any interesting news in it.

"Aunt Harrie sends you her love," Harriott murmured, as she finished reading the last lines.

Aunt Harriott Hunt was their mother's sister, and Harriott's namesake. She was a rich, elderly widow who resided in New York, and her letters were infrequent. When very young, she had left her home in South Charleston to marry a well-to-do New Yorker, but their marriage had not been a happy one, and they had lived apart for many years before his death. Her children, two daughters, had died in early adulthood, and she kept mostly to herself in a big rambling house in Pelham with a few servants and pets.

"Anything interesting?" Charlotte asked again.

"Aunt Harrie has sent more clothes and blankets and books to our prisoners at David's Island," said Harriott. "She writes that her neighbors disapprove, and tell her that she ought to be helping their own soldiers, but Auntie told them that she would not give them aid in any way."

"Good for her," Charlotte muttered, and, after a sigh, she turned back to the window and watched the rain again.

Harriott folded the letter and looked up to remark, "You seem as gloomy as the weather this afternoon, Lottie. Were you so disappointed that Captain Mitchell was not younger and handsomer?"

Charlotte pursed her lips in something between a pout and a smile and replied, "You know me too well, Harrie."

"My romantic little sister," she laughed softly. "You have asked my advice about this romanticism of yours before, but you don't seem to have taken it. You let these beautiful dreams consume you, dear, but it would be best to occupy your mind with other things for now. There is not a suitable young man anywhere near here, and likely there will not be for a long while to come."

"Yes, I know, Harrie," she conceded irritably. "I remember all that you have advised me, and what Mama has said. Just the other day she—"

Charlotte stopped, but Harriott was curious to know what their mother had told her.

"She quoted scripture to me!" Charlotte complained. "You know the verse, I'm sure. Whatsoever things are true and honest, whatever is pure and lovely, if there be any virtue, and so on, think on these things."

"Why, Lottie, scripture is always good advice," Harriott reminded her.

"Yes, that's true, but..."

"But what?"

"Well, isn't it also written in the scriptures, that when God made the first man and the first woman, Adam and Eve, and put them in the garden of Eden, he pronounced it all *good*, did he not? Love is good and pure and lovely, therefore, and I don't know why I ought not to think of it."

"That's a very clever and self-serving use of scripture," said Harriott. "The trouble is, you hardly think of anything else, dear."

Charlotte hung her head and admitted that her sister was right.

"I shall try to do better," she murmured. "I shall try."

CHAPTER THREE

The next day, Mrs. Middleford sent a note to Captain Mitchell pressing him to keep his promise and call on the family soon with his sister. Sarah replied with polite thanks and suggested a Wednesday visit. When that time came, she and her brother took a buggy and trotted the horse over the gently rolling road to the Middleford property about a mile and a half away. As their vehicle rounded a bend in the long, winding carriage drive, they were impressed by the sight of a handsome white house on top of a hill.

A few of the early houses in Flat Rock had begun as simply framed summer homes, comfortable but not extremely large, some of the original settlers putting more value on the location and the views than the size of their dwellings, but from the settlement's beginning, grand estates were being built in the area, and multiplied over the years as Flat Rock increased in popularity. The Middleford residence was not considered a mansion by the Charlestonians, but it was a spacious, stately home, and something of a showplace, with lovely ornamental grounds and one of the most impressive, spectacular views of the mountains. The house, which was called the Briars, was a three-story, mostly wooden structure with a wide, raised piazza that wrapped around the front and two sides of the first floor, its upper two stories resting on one made of stone taken out of local quarries. It was immediately surrounded by gardens and open lawns dotted with acacia trees and shrubbery, and farther off, by woods. To the rear of the house there was some pasture land, servants' quarters, and stables and other outbuildings, and to the east, not visible from the house, ran a clear, rocky creek called Briarford Stream.

After greeting the ladies at the front steps of the piazza, Captain Mitchell complimented Mrs. Middleford on the beauty of the place.

She thanked him, but added somewhat ruefully, "I'm afraid you do not see it at its best, Captain. To our eyes, it is rather run down since the war began. We cannot devote much time and money to flower gardens and things which are luxuries. Of necessity we are more concerned these days with our grove of fruit trees, our livestock, and our vegetable gardens."

From the piazza, the Middlefords and their guests enjoyed the magnificent view of the mountainous countryside, and Sarah expressed her envy as they all stood together and admired the scenery. It was a breezy day, and the winds moved broken masses of gray and white clouds across the high sun, casting moving shadows over the trees, grounds, and distant mountains. Not far from the piazza, in the shade of a massive hemlock tree, two boys were busy playing with a big black and white dog. These were Mrs. Middleford's grandsons, Gabriel and Turquand.

A brief survey of the vegetable gardens followed, after which everyone made their way to the parlor for tea. The enjoyment of tea was not a common occurrence in the household; like most other luxuries (and even many necessities), the war had made the beverage scarce and very expensive, but Mrs. Middleford had preserved a small quantity of black tea for just such special occasions. As they walked into the parlor, the captain noticed a table by a window where there were brushes, paints, and a little watercolor sketch as yet unfinished. He walked over to take a closer look, and asked who the artist in the family was.

"Oh, that is Harriott's handiwork, Captain," Louisa quickly piped up. "Don't you think it very fine?"

"It is no common talent that I see," he replied after a pause, eyeing a small painting of the Middleford house. His sister came to his side, studied it too, and agreed with his assessment.

"You are too kind," Harriott demurred, somewhat embarrassed by their praise.

"But we are not!" Sarah protested. "My brother does not flatter, and you ought to give weight to his opinion, for he is an artist himself and, I assure you, a very good one."

"Really!" cried Mrs. Middleford, intrigued. "You must tell us more about that, Captain Mitchell."

"I am but an amateur, Mrs. Middleford," he said, "but I like to paint landscapes, and seascapes. I thought once I might make it my avocation, however, my father wished otherwise."

"James has painted two beautiful views of forts Sumter and Moultrie," Sarah informed the ladies proudly. "They were much admired in Charleston, and even General Beauregard said that they were the handsomest and truest likenesses of the subjects he had seen."

"I should like to see those paintings," said Harriott, and her mother and sisters all promptly echoed the sentiment.

"I wish it were possible ladies. I sent them to my mother's house in Camden for safekeeping. However, I hope that someday they will return to my home in Charleston."

"You must show them to us someday, Captain," Louisa insisted.

"I will certainly do so if it is in my power, Miss Louisa."

"Have you done any painting here in Flat Rock?" Harriott asked him.

"No," he replied. "I haven't any supplies, but I do find this place inspiring, especially the mountain vistas."

"Poor Harrie, she can no longer find proper paper for her art," Rebecca remarked, "so she uses old wallpaper."

"Wallpaper!" the captain repeated, surprised and amused. His sister picked up the little painting, turned it over, and saw that its reverse side was colored and patterned.

"It is wallpaper!" Sarah laughed.

"I found it in an old trunk in one of the barns," Harriott explained. "It's rather ugly paper, so I didn't think it would be put to any other use."

"You have made good use of it," Captain Mitchell commended her.

"Harrie lets us see her paintings and drawings," said Charlotte, "but she keeps her other great talent secretive."

"Then how do you know it is great?" Harriott retorted, looking displeased. Seeing this, the captain did not inquire what the talent was, though his sister did; Charlotte told Sarah that Harriott wrote stories, but would seldom share them with her family.

"We have so few books here these days, we sometimes beg her to entertain us with her stories, but she only reads those she has written for the children, so we know nothing of her serious work."

"If Harrie doesn't wish it, then you ought not to insist," Mrs. Middleford said in rebuke to her youngest.

Eager to draw attention away from herself, Harriott asked Captain Mitchell what other subjects he had painted, but before he could answer, the tea was brought in, and everyone sought their places around the table. Pointing out a comfortable chair for the captain with a gracious gesture, Mrs. Middleford inquired, had he been to Europe, Rome perhaps, to copy the masters?

* * *

Back at home that evening, as the daylight began to die, James sat out on the piazza enjoying the coolness of the air and the songs of birds and insects. His sister came out and took her usual chair beside his.

"I see why you and your husband wanted a place up here," he remarked quietly. "I like these cool evenings very much."

"You know," said Sarah, "it is not unheard of here, that even in the middle of the summer, one must sleep with a blanket or two."

"I don't mind that."

The dusk grew deeper. Against the pearly gray sky, a dark little form flitted across the yard high in the air.

"That's the first bat I've seen up here," the captain observed.

"Was it a bat? I thought it was a bird."

For a long while, brother and sister sat in quiet relaxation listening to the sounds of the evening and watching the darkening evening sky. It was a clear night, and a few stars were already peeping through.

"What a lovely evening," Sarah sighed. "All we lack is a grand mountain view like the Middlefords have. Wouldn't that be nice?"

"Very nice," he agreed. "Their house is situated very nicely."

"What do you think of the Middleford ladies, now that you have gotten to know them a little better?" she asked.

"I like them well enough," he answered with a slight shrug.

"And what do you think of Harriott M.?" Sarah pressed. "You said you thought her elegant."

The captain made an "ahem" sound and shifted a little in his chair.

"Her appearance is elegant," he said. "And her manner."

"Do you think she is plain?"

"No, I don't think so," he answered rather warily. "Why do you ask?"

"Don't you remember her letter? She described herself that way. Perhaps she considers herself plain in comparison to her pretty sisters."

"Perhaps," he echoed faintly.

"Not long ago," Sarah went on, "I asked one of them why Harriott had never married. Charlotte would not tell me much at first, but hinted at some tragic love affair of a decade past. I finally coaxed more out of her, and it turns out that Harriott, at eighteen, had been engaged to a young man in Charleston, a clergyman, who died of yellow fever just a few days before they were to be married."

"Very sad."

"Apparently, she took herself out of society for several years, and never allowed another young man to address her. She has since become what I suppose is considered an old maid, or at least that is what she called herself in the letter, you recall."

"She's not my idea of an old maid. Is she the eldest?"

"Her brother Arthur is the eldest—no, there was another sister, older than Harriott, but she died just before the war, so now Harriott is the eldest of the girls. Louisa is next. She is engaged, you know."

"No, I didn't know."

"Well, I understand she is as good as engaged—I believe that's what Harriott said—to some cousin who has been courting her for years. The other two sisters are also of marriageable age, or close to it. Charlotte is a bit flighty and foolish, and perhaps rather too young, but I think Rebecca, who is nineteen years of age, would make a fine wife," said Sarah, looking at her brother in a way that made him uncomfortable.

"A fine wife for whom?" he asked.

"For you, dear brother."

"Good heavens, Sarah," he groaned.

"What! Surely you wish to marry again someday."

"And therefore it naturally follows that I should marry Miss Rebecca Middleford?"

"Why not? She is an attractive young lady from a very fine family. Next to Louisa, she is the prettiest of the daughters. Everyone thinks so."

"Just what would a pretty girl of nineteen want with me?"

"And what is wrong with you?" Sarah responded indignantly.

"Dear sister," he laughed softly, "I know I am *not* the stuff that the dreams of young maidens are made of."

* * *

Mrs. Middleford had taken a great liking to Captain Mitchell and assured him that he was welcome at their home as often as he wished to visit. She missed the company of men, especially young men, and the presence of even one in the community gave her a greater sense of security. All the other gentlemen in Flat Rock were sixty or older. Among the poorer classes in the area, those whom the Middlefords called the "country people," there were a few middle-aged men who had somehow managed to avoid military service, but they gave Mrs. Middleford no sense of protection, and she did not put much trust in them; many of the country folk resented the rich Charlestonians and their negroes, and some were known to have aided and abetted the Tories in various ways.

When Captain Mitchell next visited the Briars one afternoon, he drove over alone in his sister's buggy. Mrs. Middleford suggested that he might set up an easel and paint the view from their piazza, but he politely reminded her that he had no supplies. Her daughters were occupied with chores and letter writing and cloth making at the time of his arrival, so the mother had his company to herself for a good while before the youngest three girls made an appearance in the parlor. As the time of the evening meal approached, Mrs. Middleford invited the captain to dine with them, but he declined. Before leaving however, he informed her that he had a commission from his sister to ask a favor. During their previous visit, Sarah had noticed some unusually handsome ivy on a trellis in their garden, and wondered if she could have some cuttings to root for her own yard.

Mrs. Middleford went to the door that looked out on the garden and spoke to an elderly black man working there. For a number of years, no work had been expected of old Washington, who was approaching his nineties, but he was happiest in the garden, and was allowed to tend the ornamental plants he loved, abler hands being required for the cultivation of the vegetable gardens and other necessary chores.

"My man Wash will oblige you, Captain Mitchell," she said, gesturing toward the gardener.

James thanked her and went out to collect his sister's cuttings. As he waited for the old gardener to get them for him, he saw Miss Harriott walking in his direction. She was wearing a veil of netting over a straw hat, and long, thick yellow gloves that were a little too large for her hands. She removed the gloves, and when she raised the veil, she saw the captain standing with his cane at the edge of the garden.

"Bee keeping, Miss Harriott?" he inquired.

"Not very well, I'm afraid," she replied. "It is a new venture for me. Honey would be such a wonderful treat."

"A delightful thought. I hope you are successful."

"I am trying!"

"Your mother has been kind enough to allow my sister cuttings of some of your ivy that she fancies."

"Oh, we have plenty of it. She is welcome to them."

A young maid named Lilah came out to the piazza and asked Harriott if she had seen "the Turk." It was supper time, and he was not in the house.

"I saw him just now," she answered. "He was walking this way, and should be home soon."

The captain glanced over Harriott's shoulder, and she turned to see her nephew trudging up a hill, a gangling, horse-faced teenage boy with light brown hair like her own.

"That is the Turk?" he asked.

"Yes, that is my nephew. His name is Turquand, but everyone calls him Turk, and after you get to know him, Captain Mitchell, you will understand why. I believe he has been fishing most of the day—that is one of his favorite pastimes—but we never know just what else he may be up to."

"How old is he?"

"Fourteen, but he wishes he were sixteen, so that he could at least be allowed to serve in the home guard in South Carolina."

The boy had been fishing for many long hours on Baring's Pond, and had afterwards engaged in rough-housing and racing with some servant boys and a neighbor until he was nearly exhausted. When Turk noticed that he was being observed, he began staggering and flailing his arms in exaggerated distress. He reeled in their direction and threw himself into Harriott's arms, making her stagger to keep her balance.

"You are late for supper," she scolded him.

"Oh!" wailed the boy. "I am so tired, Auntie, and so hungry! I think I shall collapse before I reach the house."

"Well, then, you must crawl to the table," his aunt suggested humorously.

"No pity! No pity for me!" he sighed loudly and histrionically, laying his head against her shoulder.

Captain Mitchell was smiling broadly at the boy's antics, and for a fleeting moment, Harriott admired his face, which she thought quite pleasant-looking when he smiled.

"Are you so tired that you have lost all your manners?" she asked Turk. "We have a guest. This is Captain Mitchell."

The boy instantly perked up at the word *captain*.

"I'm pleased to make your acquaintance, Master Turquand," said James, offering his hand.

Turk put out a hand, but it was so filthy that his aunt immediately interdicted the gesture and apologized for him.

"Are you on furlough, Captain?" asked Turk.

"Captain Mitchell is recovering from a wound," Harriott quickly explained.

"Oh, that is grand! Will you tell me about the battles you have seen?" Turk asked him eagerly.

"Certainly."

"Hurrah! I have been longing to talk with soldiers, especially officers. There is no one to talk to here except ladies and children and old gentlemen. I will show you my sketches of some battles I read about in the papers, and you can tell me if I have imagined them correctly."

"You are an artist then, Turk," James remarked, nodding and looking impressed.

"He really is," Harriott answered for him. "You ought to show Captain Mitchell your paintings of birds. They are quite beautiful, Captain, especially the ones depicting live birds. Most of them depict the day's shooting victims though, I'm afraid."

"There is good shooting about here," Turk informed him. "Could we go out together sometime?"

James declined the invitation on account of his leg, but supposed that fishing might be a possibility.

"Your aunt tells me that you like to fish," he said. "I imagine I could do that with you."

"Hurrah!" cried Turk. "And while we fish, you can tell me about the battles, and how you got your wound. Could we do that?"

"I don't see why not," James replied.

Still hugging his aunt, Turk hurrahed again and gleefully squeezed her tighter, making her give a little laughing cry.

"Oh, I love my Auntie!" he exulted. "She is the best lady of all the ladies. She is my most favorite. And now she has brought me a soldier!"

Suddenly re-energized, Turk let go of Harriott and bounded across the yard to the house, where his supper was waiting.

* * *

The following week, Captain Mitchell and his sister visited the Middlefords again, and after that, they regularly called on the family at least twice a week, and frequently more often. Sometimes the captain visited by himself. He had found little to do in Flat Rock, and was somewhat frustrated with the slow pace of his recovery, but he tried to be of help to his sister and others, and walked each day for exercise, to strengthen his legs. He also found some diversion in his new young friend.

A few days after he made the acquaintance of Harriott's nephew Turquand, the boy appeared at the Stiles' place one morning ready to spend time fishing with the captain.

"I haven't fished your pond," he announced. "Shall we try it?"

He had brought all the necessary gear, and set about digging for worms and hunting for crickets while the captain carefully made his way down the hill to the pond with the aid of his cane.

Turk was anxious to hear about his military exploits, and seemed more interested in his stories than the fishing, but after two hours of angling and conversation they came away from the pond with a respectable catch.

Before they parted, the boy asked eagerly, "May we go fishing again soon?"

"Why, certainly Turk," said the captain. "It was a very enjoyable morning. Come again soon without fail, and I'll tell you about General Beauregard."

"Oh, Beauregard!" he cried. "He is my hero! I shall come again soon without fail. May I call two days from now?"

"You may. We'll fish together often."

From that time forward, Turk's appearance at the Stiles' place was as regular as the captain's visits to the Middleford household. A friendship developed between the two, and Captain Mitchell found himself growing very fond of the boy as well as the whole family.

CHAPTER FOUR

One week, a pattern of weather set in that brought sudden changes each day, and for several days there were showers or thunderstorms in the mornings or afternoons, followed by a clearing in the evenings. During this time, Captain Mitchell and his sister were invited to the Middleford's house for supper one evening, but the rain delayed their departure until dusk, and they arrived at the Briars with apologies for their lateness.

"Oh, we quite understand that the rain kept you," said Mrs. Middleford, greeting her guests at the door. "We have waited for you — well, everyone except the boys. They have had their supper and gone upstairs to bathe."

A lovely table was laid out in the dining room, and after all the ladies sat down the captain took a seat opposite Harriott . The food was plain and not abundant, but it was good, nourishing fare, and even included chicken that night. Relishing the meat, which was not regularly part of their diet, the girls remembered a time during the previous winter when chickens had been very scarce, and laughed about the day that one of the valuable birds had to be slaughtered when Charlotte was ill.

"Mama insisted that Lottie must have some chicken broth to

strengthen her," said Harriott, "but oh, how she agonized over the killing of that one chicken, thinking how many eggs and chicks were being sacrificed with it! The poor dear was almost in tears, thinking, I suppose, that we might all starve."

"Ah, yes," said Mrs. Middleford, smiling and laughing a little. "I recall that I was somewhat consoled when Turk said to me, oh, Grandmama, it was only a rooster."

After the meal, another seldom-seen delicacy appeared on the table, a pound cake, and Mrs. Middleford cut the pieces herself and passed them out on small china plates. As everyone enjoyed dessert, the quiet of the evening was suddenly disturbed by a loud, alarming sound which seemed to originate just outside the house.

Sarah was so startled that she dropped her fork, and Mrs. Middleford made a great inhalation and put a hand to her heart. All the women were wide-eyed.

"Good heavens!" the older lady exclaimed. "A wild animal is out there!"

"It sounded like a wild cat," Louisa gasped.

Captain Mitchell rose from his chair and went to the door, where he took his pistol out of the holster hanging on the coat rack.

"Don't worry, ladies," he reassured them, while Charlotte began lamenting that their dog Josh might be in danger, and all the livestock. The captain opened the door, stepped out and closed it behind him. From the piazza he surveyed the yard, which was illuminated by a waxing gibbous moon just risen. The alarming sound came to his ears again, and at the same moment, he saw some movement next to a large oak tree, and then another sound, this time that of a human voice. Instantly he recognized the muffled laughter of Turk.

Captain Mitchell went out to the piazza and, leaning on his cane as usual, descended the steps and walked briskly to the nearby tree, where the boy was doubled over in helpless mirth.

"So you're the wild animal," the captain observed sarcastically.

"Did I scare 'em?" Turk wheezed.

"Yes, you did. You made quite a convincing wild cat."

"I've been practicing!"

"You ought to be ashamed of yourself. Don't you think your family has enough to frighten and concern them without your pranks?"

The captain tried to sound stern as he reproached the boy, but he was suppressing a smile.

"You will now come inside with me, young man, and confess what you have done."

"I won't!" laughed Turk.

"You will."

The captain took the culprit by the arm and propelled him across the yard, up the steps, and into the house.

"Here's your wild cat," he announced inside, while Turk covered his face and quivered with laughter.

"Young scamp!" his grandmother cried angrily. "Go up to your bed! If your grandfather were here he would take a strap to you!"

Unrepentant, and still tittering, the boy lurched over to the stairs and began going up, pretending he was tripping and falling up each step. The captain returned to his seat at the table.

"Oh, that boy!" fumed Louisa. "As if we did not have enough to try our nerves!"

"He delights in aggravation," Rebecca complained.

Harriott was biting her lips to hide a smile, but when she saw that Captain Mitchell was doing the same, and looking into her eyes with merriment he could not hide, both of them burst into laughter.

"I beg your pardon, ladies," he apologized, seeing that the others were not amused.

"I don't think it is funny to frighten people out of their wits," Mrs. Middleford said indignantly.

Harriott and the captain simultaneously assumed a contrite, subdued demeanor after this remark, and then seemed to turn all their attention to the few bites of cake left on their plates.

* * *

A few days later, Captain Mitchell was again a guest at the Middleford house, arriving at dusk after another rainy afternoon. His sister was feeling unwell that evening and had not accompanied him. After supper, everyone was assembled in the parlor, where Louisa played a few tunes on the piano, and Rebecca then read poetry aloud while her sisters knitted and sewed. Turk was stretched out on a settee with a book, blithely ignoring everyone else, and his little brother Gabriel was lolling in a nearby chair with a toy.

Gabriel was a blonde, spindly boy of nine. He had the long, narrow Middleford face, and was as angelic in looks and disposition as his brother Turquand was impish, but he was a sensitive child, and his health was delicate. As his cousin began reading her second poem, Gabriel interrupted to complain of a stomach ache, and Lilah the maid, who was also his nurse, was soon summoned to take him upstairs to bed.

After reciting several poems in succession, Rebecca paused to take a drink of water and turn the pages of her book to find the next selections. During the relative quiet of these moments, a low but distinct noise was heard by everyone—a kind of scraping or rustling from outside. It grew more pronounced, and the sisters looked from one to the other in perplexity. Mrs. Middleford had just been dozing off in her easy chair, and her head abruptly bobbed up.

"What is that?" she asked irritably. "Turk is up to his tricks again!"

"I am right here, Grandmama!" the boy protested. "How can it be me?"

"Has it grown windy this evening?" Harriott wondered. "Perhaps it's only the wind blowing the bushes about."

Captain Mitchell got up from his chair and walked over to a window. The moon was still nearly full and very bright, and he saw no movement in the shrubbery and trees.

"There is no wind tonight," he said.

"What if someone is in the bushes near the house?" Louisa ventured fearfully.

"Surely it is only Josh, or some pig that has got loose," Harriott suggested.

"Josh is penned up tonight, and so are the pigs," Turk informed her, casting a casual glance toward the window just behind the settee where he was lounging.

"Well, go and let Josh out," warbled his grandmother. "Isn't he a watch dog?"

"Allow me, Mrs. Middleford," Captain Mitchell offered, opening the door.

Outside, the night was very quiet except for the chirping of crickets. The captain leaned on his cane and gazed around for a while, then went to the dog's pen, which was close to the house. Josh seemed glad to be let loose, and, thinking that a night hunt might be on, began sniffing and circling around, expectant of some command. When Captain Mitchell went back inside, leaving him on the piazza, the animal seemed disappointed, and sat down resignedly to wait and hope for some development that might involve the dog of the house.

"I see nothing moving out there," Captain Mitchell announced. "I believe I would have seen anything amiss in such moonlight."

"Was Josh out?" asked Harriott.

"Not until I let him out. It may have been a small animal making those sounds—something harmless, I'm sure."

As soon as he finished speaking, the same strange noise they had all heard earlier occurred again.

"Why doesn't Josh go after the thing?" Rebecca fretted. "He doesn't even bark!"

"Maybe—maybe it's some critter with hydrophobia," Turk suggested ominously, with a flash of impishness that was not lost on Captain Mitchell.

"Oh! Then Josh musn't go after it!" Charlotte insisted. "Let him in the house, won't you Captain Mitchell?"

"Do you wish it, Mrs. Middleford?" he asked.

"Well, no. But if you would put the animal back in his pen, I think he would be safe there."

"That is wise. Best not to let him in the house," the captain agreed. "I shall do as you ask, and if the company will excuse me, I think I shall take myself home now, while there is still enough moonlight. I noticed that clouds were beginning to gather when I went out just now."

"Oh, I shall be more afraid when you leave us," Rebecca lamented. "But of course you ought to go, if you must."

"You do disappoint us, Captain," said Mrs. Middleford, "but I quite understand. It is really not good for anyone to travel after dark these days."

"I am armed," he reminded her. "Please forgive me, ladies. I'm sure you have nothing to fear tonight. Isn't that right, Turk?"

"We—ll," drawled the boy. "I don't rightly know about that."

Captain Mitchell studied Turk for a few moments with a slight smile that his mustache concealed. The ladies said their "good nights" to him, and after a few more pleasantries, he was on his way. Soon they heard the wheels of his buggy crushing over some gravel in the driveway, and listened in silence until the sound died away completely. Within the next minute, the silence was broken again by the rustling noise outside, and this time it was louder than ever.

Louisa jumped up from her seat.

"I am going to see what it is!" she declared in frustrated excitement.

"You certainly will do no such thing!" her mother commanded. "Sit down, Louisa! Turk, take your gun and go out and see what you can find."

The boy rolled his eyes.

"If Captain Mitchell couldn't find anything, how do you expect that I will?" he whined.

"If it is an animal, Josh ought to have scented it," said Harriott. "Indeed, he ought to scent—it."

She had stopped herself before she involved the word "Tory."

After a few minutes passed, the noise occurred yet again, causing general consternation. The ladies made all kinds of exclamations, but could not settle on what to do. Finally, Harriott came up with the idea of getting the manservant Jeffrey to see about the recurring, puzzling disturbance outside. Turk was asked to go and find him, but the boy refused to leave the house.

"What if it gets me!" he said indignantly. "I'll be foaming at the mouth directly!"

"Well, for heaven's sake," Harriott grumbled. "I will go and find Jeffrey."

She rose, pushed away her chair, and had almost reached the door when Turk suddenly gave a loud, piercing cry of pain and fear, bringing her to an abrupt halt. The boy suddenly sat up, twisting his head and body toward the window and looking down frantically at his left arm, most of which was concealed behind the settee.

Moments later, footsteps were heard outside, followed by a knock at the door, and a familiar voice said, "It is I, ladies. Do not be alarmed."

Harriott opened the door and Captain Mitchell stepped in.

"We heard you drive off!" Rebecca exclaimed, startled to see him, like everyone else. "But we heard no carriage returning!"

"Did you have an accident?" Harriott inquired, puzzled.

"No, I only drove a short ways off. I came back on foot to find a culprit," he explained. He walked directly over to Turk, took hold of the boy's left arm, and lifted it up so that the ladies could see a string that was tied to his wrist.

"This string," said the captain, "is attached to the tall bushes below the window, which is partly open. *That* is the noise you have been hearing."

Turk was beginning to shake with laughter, while all his female relations fumed and scolded him.

"How—how did you know?" he asked Captain Mitchell, still wheezing with mirth.

"I was a boy once, too," was the reply.

"Well, Captain, you gave Turk a fright in return, and it serves him right," said Harriott.

"I was *not* frightened!" Turk declared.

"Oh yes you were," Harriott retorted. "We all saw your face when the string was pulled."

"It hurt!"

"Oh, did it hurt you?" said the captain, with sardonic sympathy.

"Ha, ha! You were positively terrified!" gloated Charlotte, happy to exact a little revenge on her mischievous cousin.

"Serves you right," Rebecca hissed at him.

* * *

The next morning, Captain Mitchell woke to an aching leg. He had overexerted himself at the Briars the night before, and was now paying a price for it, so he rested as much as possible that day. After a good night's sleep, he felt much better, and in the late afternoon, he decided to take his usual walk.

About the same time he left his sister's house, Harriott also went out for a walk, partly for the exercise, but mainly to seek solace. The family had received a letter from her brother Arthur that day, and she was feeling anxious for him once again. She made her way to the church, which was empty, and went to her family's pew.

It was a warm day, but it was comfortable inside the church. The bright hot July sunlight that had reigned much of the morning was muted and tempered by the colors of the thick stained glass windows, and the stone walls and floors imparted a coolness to the air. Harriott kneeled on the prayer cushion for a long while, her face lowered against her clasped hands on the back of the pew. She was concentrating so deeply on her murmured prayers that she did not hear the faint creaking of the big wooden door at the back of the church, but she brought herself bolt upright, startled, when a tapping sound came to her ears. She turned and saw Captain Mitchell with his cane. He paused and gave a slight bow.

"You are here alone, Miss Middleford?" he asked. "I am surprised."

"I sometimes come here by myself," she explained. "I was praying for my brother."

She rose from her knees and took a seat on the pew.

"And I have interrupted your prayers," he said apologetically.

"I didn't mean to stay much longer, so there is no harm done."

The captain gazed all around the church appreciatively.

"I was told this was a lovely chapel," he remarked. "I was walking, and thought I might look inside to see if that was true, and perhaps say a prayer or two myself."

Harriott told him that their church had been built in the style of an English country chapel. He commented on the architecture, admiring in particular the handsome wooden beams and arches overhead. They talked of the windows and other architectural details, and as they talked, the last narrow shaft of sunlight shining in through the open doorway disappeared; eventually, the light in the church dimmed considerably, and they could hear the wind beginning to rustle the trees and leaves outside.

"It has been clouding up," said Captain Mitchell. "I think another rain storm is brewing."

"Then I ought to go home," said Harriott, getting to her feet.

"Permit me to walk with you. I do not like to think of a lady walking here alone."

She nodded her consent to his request and they left the church together. The sun shone out briefly as they began their way down the path, though it was soon obscured again by the dark rain clouds gathering overhead.

"It is so beautiful here," the captain remarked, admiring the trees and thickets all around them. "I scarcely expected to enjoy myself this much when I came here to stay with my sister, but the weather here is so superior to Charleston, the mountains are splendid, and the company very agreeable."

"Except for the Tories," said Harriott.

"Yes, except for them," he agreed.

His expression grew more serious. "I expect the Tories will only grow bolder, Miss Harriott, and that things will be worse for all of you in Flat Rock. You and your family ought to consider going elsewhere, I think. I shall send my sister to Camden when I leave here."

"We have talked of leaving Flat Rock, but Papa is so indecisive about whether and where we ought to go. I think the decision will have to be made by Mama, though she is not accustomed to making such decisions for us. Greenville or Columbia seem the most likely choices for us."

"Greenville seems a fine choice to me. I can't think of anywhere else safer for you."

Halfway through the stroll back to the Middleford house, Harriott noticed that the captain's limp had become more pronounced. He paused to rest, admiring a lush, vivid green expanse of ferns that covered a shady area near the foot of a hill.

"Would you like to paint that scene?" asked Harriott.

"It's lovely, but no," he said.

"There is no drama in it, as there is the scene of a fort, or a stormy landscape," she suggested.

"Yes, that's part of it. No romance, I suppose."

"What would you add to the scene to make it more interesting?"

"Oh, I don't know. Perhaps a beautiful damsel, or a knight upon a steed."

"Very romantic notions," she observed, amused.

"Perhaps it's my recent reading," he laughed. "My sister's meager library mainly consists of Spenser and Tennyson."

They walked on, and a little while later, Harriott heard the captain make a faint sigh of pain when he stumbled a little over a rock. He saw her look of concern.

"I believe I have overestimated my strength, and the soundness of my limb," he remarked with a slight grimace.

"May I be of help to you?" she offered. "Perhaps if you leaned on me a little…my shoulder."

He hesitated.

"No one will think it improper," she assured him. "Besides, there is no one about to see."

"Well, perhaps I might give it a try."

He put his arm around her shoulders, but tried not to shift much of his weight to her.

"There," she said. "Does that help?"

"Yes, I believe it does a little."

As they passed by a spot that had a view of the faraway mountains, Captain Mitchell commented again on the beauty of the country.

"You know," he went on, "my uncle's plantation on Charleston neck is a very beautiful place. It is on the Cooper River, and has some of the most superb, graceful oak trees I have ever seen. But I have grown so fond of this place, I almost think it equally beautiful."

"Isn't it?" she agreed. "I love it here. Before the war, it was a kind of paradise to me. I can still take refuge in its beauty, though I must say it does not soothe me as it used to. There is too much trouble for me to be at peace."

"You worry about your brother," he observed.

"My brother, several uncles, and a multitude of cousins and friends. We have already lost quite a few of them."

"I haven't any brothers, thank God, but like you I have lost kinsmen and friends. It is the same story with everyone, I imagine."

"Yes, the same sad story," Harriott lamented. "There is to be another soldier's funeral here soon. Have you heard of it?"

"My sister mentioned it to me."

"The Count de Clemonte's son. His two sisters will bury him tomorrow. We shall attend the services."

"Who is this Count?" he asked.

Harriott explained that the gentleman was a nobleman of the old regime who had fled France many years ago when it grew too dangerous there for the Royalists. The Count eventually became the French consul at Charleston, and like so many other residents, had left the city when he feared that the Yankees would capture it. He and his family then took refuge in their summer home in Flat Rock, a beautiful, unusual house that resembled a French chateau. His son Charles, an officer of a regiment of Louisiana Zouaves, had been killed in battle in Virginia.

"The old Count was a widower of many years," Harriott continued, "but recently he married a very beautiful young lady and returned to France with her, and I'm afraid he left his two unmarried daughters without sufficient support. They had to give up their fine house here, and live now on a very modest, small place near ours, and keep a school for girls."

"My sister knows those ladies," said the captain. "She has plans to attend the funeral."

"Will you accompany her?"

"Perhaps. I suppose I ought to, out of respect for a fellow soldier, if nothing else."

When they reached the edge of the yard Captain Mitchell removed his arm from her, and they paused. A few drops of rain were now falling.

"Won't you come in?" Harriott asked him. "I think you ought to rest, and I shouldn't like to think of you being caught in bad weather."

Finding her persuasive, he accepted her invitation, and they crossed the yard and went into the house. As the afternoon wore on, the weather only grew worse, and developed into a thunder storm. The storm passed, but a steady rain continued, and the captain was invited to spend the night at the Briars. When Mrs. Middleford offered to send her man Jeffrey to Mrs. Stiles' house to inform her that her brother would not be home that night, and to act as her protector during his absence, Captain Mitchell agreed to stay over.

That evening Turk was banished from polite company for his latest infraction, and stayed upstairs with Gabriel. It had grown somewhat cool and damp inside the house, and Mrs. Middleford ordered a little fire to be made in the parlor, where she and her daughters sat with their guest. The ladies were preoccupied with the funeral that was to take place the next morning, and talked of the Clemonte sisters and their father the count, deploring the fact that he had returned to France and left them to fend for themselves in Flat Rock.

"How terrible for the ladies," Louisa observed sadly. "Their father so far away, and now their brother, taken from them forever. They must feel quite alone in the world. Their neighbor, Mrs. Lowndes, says they have taken to their beds in grief. The poor dears, they had hoped that their brother would recover from his wounds, but in his last letter, he told them otherwise. Poor Beatrice allowed Mrs. Lowndes to read the letter, and she found it most touching. Charles wrote that he was willing to die, and that he was happy to give his life in such a sacred cause. The last words of his letter were, 'I go to join our dear mother.'"

Mrs. Middleford closed her eyes momentarily, looking deeply touched.

"So many people respected him," Harriott observed. "They

say he was a most gallant officer. We hear that General Beauregard praised him at Manassas."

"He is like so many of our young men nowadays," Mrs. Middleford remarked thoughtfully, opening her eyes to gaze at a portrait of her son that hung on the opposite wall. "I think they are infinitely superior to those of my day. These times I suppose, have brought out a certain nobility and seriousness in them, but I really think there is also a difference in nature. I don't remember a single young man of my time for whom I felt such admiration and respect, but I know of many men now who do inspire reverence."

"I don't think it is surprising," said Louisa, in the same thoughtful tone. "Every day in this war, every hour really, our men stand face to face with the unseen world—eternity itself."

"That's true," Rebecca concurred. "Any day, any hour might be that of their death."

"Do you agree, Captain?" asked Mrs. Middleford, turning to him. "We have observed these things in the men we know, and what we read of them in letters and reports, but you have been in our army, and have seen much more of it with your own eyes."

The captain pondered a little while before answering.

"I have seen men such as you have described, Mrs. Middleford," he said. "I have seen good, and bad. At the beginning of the war, most of the young men I knew, especially the youngest of military age, enlisted in the army out of patriotism, with an admirable idealism added to it. Unfortunately, some of them imagined soldiering to be a glorious adventure, but once they got a real taste of military life, endured its tedium, hardships, and dangers long enough, some turned to comforts and diversions that could not be called noble. And then there were—. "

"We heard of respectable young gentlemen gambling at cards!" Rebecca interjected, with a severe look of disapproval.

A smile came to Captain Mitchell's lips which he quickly straightened out.

"Well, yes," he said. "There were young men who were taken out of homes where they would not likely have been exposed to such temptations."

"That is why Mama frets so much about Arthur, besides the danger he is in," said Rebecca. "She worries that a Christian young man might be led astray."

"Any man might be led astray, Miss Rebecca," the captain replied. "What is it the scriptures say—that the devil roams about like a prowling lion, seeking whom he may devour?"

"He cannot devour a Christian," Rebecca declared confidently.

"But I have seen many a Christian bearing his teeth marks," said the captain. "I have a few myself."

"I think we did not allow you to finish your answer to Mama's question," Harriott put in apologetically. "Please, do go on as you intended, Captain Mitchell."

"I think I was going to say," he went on, "that there were many men, young and old, who were earnest and sound in their character and beliefs, and who had nothing to fear in death. There were others who were not so serious-minded, but once some of these young men got into the real fighting, and saw the true horrors of war, saw their comrades dying on the battlefield and in the hospital...once they saw all these things, many did undergo a change. Whether it was from hearing a chaplain's sermon, reading a Bible, or a tract, or letters from mothers, fathers, or wives troubled for their spiritual welfare, they came to see that other world, the unseen world as you called it, Miss Louisa, and acted accordingly. When such a young man died, his chaplain or his officer could at least write to his loved ones, that his soul was safe."

Mrs. Middleford thought of a cousin's son who had recently died of his wounds in a Richmond hospital.

"Young Mason," she recalled sadly, "a cousin of ours, was such a young man. His mother was with him as he died, and said he was in perfect peace, knowing that his sins were forgiven. A peaceful death, full of faith, as she described it in her letter to me."

She looked off again at the portrait of her son, then cast her eyes down toward the floor in troubled, private meditations. Everyone fell silent for a few moments with their own similar reflections, until the quiet and seriousness of the moment was interrupted by a shriek from an upper floor. Soon little Gabriel came tramping down the stairs in a nightshirt, crying and whimpering about some mistreatment by his brother.

"Is Turk making up things to frighten you again?" his aunt Charlotte asked.

The boy nodded, pouting and wiping away tears.

"It's bad little boys who should be frightened, not good ones," Rebecca said indignantly.

"Come to your auntie," Harriott coaxed him. "Come and sit with me."

The boy ran over to her and climbed up into her lap. He cheered up immediately, enclosed in the warmth of her shawl, and his bright little presence caused the company's conversation to be channeled into lighter topics for the rest of the evening.

About ten o'clock, Mrs. Middleford rose and made it known that she meant to retire for the evening. Her daughters seemed inclined to do the same, and Captain Mitchell thought it proper to follow their example. Mrs. Middleford showed him to a cozy guest room across the hall from the parlor, and as he closed the door, he saw Charlotte and Rebecca going upstairs with their mother, and also heard Louisa saying goodnight.

CHAPTER FIVE

After Captain Mitchell lay down in his bed and closed his eyes, not bothering to undress except to remove his coat and shoes, he began to hear a low murmur of conversation from the parlor. Apparently, not everyone had gone to bed. He soon discerned that one of the voices belonged to Gabriel. The only other one he heard, a soft, female voice, was that of Miss Harriott. A few minutes passed, and the murmur continued. The sound of their conversation did not disturb him, but for some reason, he felt restless, and not being sleepy in the least, he decided to go out and join in it, and sat up to put his shoes on.

In the parlor, he found Harriott now seated in her mother's easy chair before the hearth, with Gabriel still sprawled across her lap.

"May I join you?" asked the captain, glancing toward the other chair that faced the fireplace. "I find I am not sleepy at all."

"Please do," she replied. "I hope our talking did not disturb you."

"Not at all."

Harriott's nephew tried to say something, but was checked by a great yawn.

"Gabriel is wanting a bedtime story now," she explained. "He says he shall not go to bed tonight without one."

"Auntie Harrie, tell me the funny story about the bed bugs again," begged the child. "Please, please!"

"Yes, do tell it," Captain Mitchell encouraged her. "I'd like to hear something amusing."

"Well," Harriott began in an exhalation, after which she drew in a deep breath and began her tale. "When I was a little girl, the journey from Charleston to Flat Rock was rather more arduous than it is now. There was no railroad then, even part of the way. We travelled by coach, and had to stop at inns along the way. Quite often, these places of accommodation were very poor. The houses at which travelers were promised entertainment for man and beast were fit much of the time only for the comfort of the latter."

Her nephew giggled at this and squirmed in her lap, obviously anticipating some detail that was to follow.

"There were many annoyances in these places," she went on. "Beds full of bugs, and nearly every meal served to the tune of—"

"Chicken, chicken, chicken!" cried the boy, throwing up his arms.

"He knows the story well," the captain observed laughingly.

Harriott nodded and continued, "We learned to bring some of our own food, and pillows, and camphor to keep away the bugs, but some inexperienced travellers were not so well prepared. On one of our journeys, as we entered an inn, we heard a gentleman from Kentucky complaining of the bugs to the lady tavern keeper. The good woman indignantly vowed that she had not a single bug in her house. No, ma'am says the Kentuckian, that is true, you have not a *single* bug—they are all married, with large families!"

This was the part Gabriel liked the best, and as usual it brought on peals of boyish laughter. Captain Mitchell seemed delighted, too, and laughed heartily.

"Now that you have had your story, it is time for bed, Gabriel," Harriott told him.

"Oh, let me stay with you for just a little while," he pleaded, yawning again.

"Very well," she consented. "But just for a little while."

Gabriel snuggled closer to her, closed his eyes, and in a little while, he had fallen asleep.

"I wish I could go to sleep so quickly and easily," the captain remarked in a quiet voice.

"So do I," Harriott agreed.

He watched the dying fire for a while in silence, then remarked, "Your sister Miss Rebecca tells me you are always writing something."

"Oh, I write in my spare moments," said Harriott.

"She says you read your stories to the children, and that they enjoy them very much. Was that one of your stories you were telling Gabriel?"

"No, not one of mine. It was something I remember from my girlhood."

"Do you write other things?" he wondered. "Things not meant for children?

"For the most part, yes. I have written only a few stories that children might like. I tried poetry, but I found it too difficult. I like prose better now, and so I write stories. Someday I should like to write something more substantial."

"I should like to read something of yours," he said, "but your sister says you are very secretive about your serious work, so I don't imagine you would allow it."

"Oh, no! I'm afraid you might find my writing too naïve and…perhaps otherworldly, as my sisters call it."

"I don't think you are naïve, Miss Harriott. Are you otherworldly?"

"Mama says I live too much in dreams."

"Oh, that just means you have a strong imagination. I like imaginative people. But I think your sisters mean to pay you a compliment by calling you otherworldly. I think they mean you are spiritual, and they tell me they wish they could be stronger in that way, as you are."

"I am not so spiritual as they imagine me, Captain, I assure you. And if I am, it is because I am weak, not strong."

Returning to the subject of writing, they began to talk of authors and works of literature, and their likes and dislikes among them. That subject eventually led to another topic, travel, and they shared their various experiences and observations abroad. Reminiscing about Italy, both agreed that Florence was the city they preferred above all others there. Architecture had been the captain's primary interest at the time he visited Florence, and he fondly recalled making sketches of the Duomo, a place she remembered well. Then they spoke of the paintings and other works of art they had seen at the Galleria dell'Accademia, Harriott expressing a preference for the beauty and reverence of sacred subjects.

She was curious about Captain Mitchell as an artist, and asked him about his work.

"Tell me about your paintings," she said. "Your sister said you had painted forts Sumter and Moultrie. Tell me about Sumter first. Did you paint it before the bombardment?"

He thought for a few moments, casting back in his memory more than three years, to the last month of 1860.

"I had just started work on my painting of Sumter at the time of the secession convention in Charleston," he began. "I made a sketch, and meant to show it in a bright daylight scene, but after the

Federals occupied the fort, I changed my mind, and began painting a darker picture. After that, there was such a sense of foreboding about the place. That massive, powerful structure in the harbor, was to me like an evil omen, so I painted it in the sanguinary light of a sunset against a fiery, cloudy sky."

"I can just imagine it as you describe it," Harriott remarked, a little wide-eyed, remembering the fort, which she had seen many times, and such evening skies in Charleston.

"You would not recognize Sumter now, Miss Harriott. It is a ruin, though it still defends the harbor."

"And what of Moultrie?" she asked. "Tell me of that painting."

"Ah, Moultrie—well, it is full of light," he said, and went on to describe his depiction of the fort as it appeared in April 1861.

They talked for nearly two hours, while gradually, imperceptibly, the fire died down, until there was only one small flickering tongue of flame rising above the glowing, pulsating embers. The captain asked Harriott if she wished him to put more wood in the fireplace.

After a moment's hesitation, and a glance at a mantle clock, she replied, "I really ought to put Gabriel to bed. It is nearly midnight."

"Ah," he said, "I was afraid you would say that. It is so peaceful and pleasant here...with you, and your slumbering colt. Will you wake him?"

"I must. I cannot carry such a horse!" she laughed softly.

"Let me carry him," the captain offered, rising to his feet— but Harriott saw him wince slightly as soon as he put weight on his injured leg.

"Perhaps you shouldn't," she suggested. "Your injury—"

"Yes, I think you are right," he agreed, a little ruefully.

"Sometimes I forget that I am lame. Talking with you, I could forget that."

She answered him with a smile and gently shook the sleeping boy by the shoulder until he opened his eyes.

"Let me stay here, Auntie," Gabriel moaned, "I am so warm and comfortable."

"It may be comfortable for you, dear, but your auntie cannot hold you all night. Now let's to bed."

The child whined and sighed, but was forced to his feet, and nodded heavily to the captain as a 'good night' as he was led away.

* * *

The following morning, one of Mrs. Middleford's servants took the captain home in a carriage, but not long afterwards, he was again in the family's company at the funeral of Charles de Clemonte.

As he walked into the church with Sarah, Captain Mitchell saw the Clemonte sisters for the first time—two thin, middle-aged ladies whose pale, solemn faces were visible behind dark, gauzy veils. They were foreign-looking faces he thought at first, but then upon further reflection, he wondered if perhaps they only appeared foreign to him because he knew they were French. Their faded mourning dresses of crepe were draped with costly black European laces, and they tottered down the aisle to a front pew on the arms of two old gentlemen. The flag of France was on display behind the pulpit that day in honor of their deceased brother.

Once the Clemonte sisters were seated, James guided his sister to a pew directly across the center aisle from the Middleford family pew, and they sat on the end closest to the aisle. It was not long before the Middleford ladies appeared, and as they filed into the row to take their seats, they all turned and nodded or whispered greetings to the captain and Mrs. Stiles.

Harriott, the last in the little procession, took the place next to the aisle, and after she finished speaking to the captain, she gazed into his eyes a few more seconds—that is, for a few more seconds longer than necessary before she looked away—and in those moments, something happened to him.

The clergyman, Reverend Reade, stepped into the pulpit, and the service began. James tried to concentrate on the words of the priest, tried to focus on the importance and solemnity of the occasion, but his attention was now divided, and he found himself thinking of Harriott and stealing glances at her, admiring her winsome, serene profile.

The elderly priest spoke movingly of Colonel Clemonte's gallant service in the army and the sacrifice he had made for a country he had come to love as his own, emphasizing that though this gentleman might have easily elected to return to his native country far away, he had instead chosen to fight in defense of the cause of "our independence and self-government." The clergyman then made use of the Frenchman's example to lead into a rather lengthy exhortation concerning steadfastness in dedication to the cause. Though acknowledging that the enemy was much greater in number and resources, the speaker reminded his listeners how the great Hebrew leader Gideon had overcome a vast Midianite army with only three hundred warriors, and the help of the Lord.

Early in the service, it began to rain, but by the time the mourners left the church to walk out to the grave site, the shower had ended, and the sun was glowing white hot behind thinning, ragged gray clouds. The only drops of water still falling to the earth were those trickling down from the roof of the church and the leaves of the trees.

Unescorted, walking arm in arm rather unsteadily, the dead man's sisters followed the pall bearers, who slowly and carefully carried their burden to an open grave and placed it on the ground at the edge of its final resting place. The metallic coffin was wrapped in a Confederate flag, and a wreath of flowers was placed at each end. A laurel wreath rested on the raised part in the middle, with a cross of green leaves and white flowers. Leaning down, the two bereaved women raised their veils and gazed on the casket containing their brother, their expressions full of somber recognition that it held only his remains—only a reminder of him— for all that really was their brother, was in another world.

"Mon frère, mon frère," one whispered brokenly. She began to weep, and the other sister put an arm around her. Mrs. Middleton also came to the grieving woman's side to support her.

The funeral service was concluded at the graveside, and after a final prayer, the mourners slowly dispersed.

Captain Mitchell took his sister's arm and leaned on her and his cane as they made their way down the terraced paths of the cemetery. Reaching the road, he helped Sarah into the buggy, while the Middleford ladies took the Clemonte sisters into their carriage and drove away.

That afternoon, as James sat alone on the piazza, he felt the same restlessness he had experienced the night before and decided to take a walk, with no particular destination in mind. He walked along at a slower pace than usual, not because of his lameness, but because he wanted time to himself, time to think, before he was in his sister's company again. His thoughts returned to Harriott, and in his mind he replayed parts of their long conversation at the Briars the night before, not so much to hear what she had to say again, but to see her face, which he had found himself studying with an artist's eye at the funeral that day. He had watched her praying in the church, and afterwards, bowing her head respectfully during the graveside service. The thought had occurred to him that it was a face he would like to paint, and he now contemplated how he might capture it in a portrait.

What a gentle, elegant, intelligent face it was, he reflected, so perfectly expressive of the inner person, and made lovely by that very spirit.

"She is lovely," he thought. "Botticelli would have chosen her as his model for an angel, or a madonna."

His steps became even slower as his concentration grew deeper, and he suddenly came to a stop when he fully realized something he had been vaguely suspecting since that morning— that he was falling in love with Harriott Middleford.

He had not been studying her with the eye of an artist, but that of a lover, and now he knew it.

Though immediately reveling in the joy of this love, he was also painfully aware of its risks. She was fond of him, he could tell, but was there hope for something more? She had lost one lover to death, he recalled—was she afraid to love again, and perhaps lose another to war? Did she have it fixed in her mind and heart that she would never take such a risk again?

Surely not, he decided. There had to be some hope, he told himself. In the church that morning, he thought he had seen something in her eyes that gave him hope.

* * *

Over the next few weeks, Captain Mitchell kept up both his regular visits to the Middlefords and his outings with young Turquand. Though he was now aware that his feelings for Harriott had become much more than friendship, he made no declaration to her, but made every effort to deepen and solidify their friendship, hoping that her affections might be undergoing a similar transformation. His soaring, hopeful spirits filled him with energy, and he found an outlet for it in long walks during an extended spell of splendid weather. His injured leg grew stronger, and all its intermittent aches and pains gradually disappeared altogether.

Once in a while, when friends and acquaintances were visiting the Briars (usually their neighbors in Flat Rock), James would manage to get Harriott to himself for a private conversation while her mother and sisters were distracted with the other guests, and she always seemed to prefer his company over theirs.

During this time it became more and more evident that Harriott was the captain's favorite among the ladies, but the family, and least of all Harriott, did not find his attentions unusual. It was nothing out of the ordinary for her to receive such approbation and compliments from the opposite sex. It was in fact common for her male relations and friends to admire her openly. The older men, her father, uncles (and, earlier in her life, grandfathers) had for many years appreciated her propriety, her good sense, and the generous, loving spirit in her that always sought and rejoiced in the happiness of others. Her brother and male cousins valued her for the same qualities, as well as her honesty and sense of humor, and one of her cousins, a young cadet, often proclaimed, only half-jokingly, that he wished he were older so that he could court Harriott, because she was "the best lady in the world."

Harriott was used to such fond looks as Captain Mitchell gave her, and put no interpretation on them other than friendship — for some reason forgetting or discounting the fact that he was a widower, and therefore an eligible man, whose admiration might indicate something beyond mere friendliness.

The captain's love for Harriott only grew stronger over these last few weeks of summer, but he kept his feelings to himself, even hiding them from his sister — until one evening in early September.

In the pleasant calm of twilight, Sarah joined her brother on the piazza. He seemed to welcome her company, but she found him preoccupied. He was not as talkative as usual, and as he gazed off into the distance, he gave the distinct impression that he was not looking at anything actually visible.

"How deep in thought you are this evening," she observed.

"Hm-m?" he said, turning to her in slow motion.

"What are you thinking of?" she asked curiously.

"Must I be thinking? Perhaps I was only observing the lovely view."

"You were thinking," she declared smugly.

A smile slowly widened across his face.

"Oh—ho!" she exulted. "I knew I was right. I know you too well, dear brother. Now tell me all about it."

He studied her with skeptical amusement.

"I don't know that I can trust you with a secret," he said.

"A secret!" she cried, her eyebrows rising high with eager interest. "Now you must tell me! You know you will not have a moment's peace with me until you do."

"You're not very good at keeping secrets," he objected teasingly.

"Oh, but I can keep yours, I promise! Don't torment me! I give you my word, I will keep your secret," she pleaded.

He laughed softly and gazed off into the distance again. She begged a little more, and he finally relented, sighing, "Oh, very well, Sarah."

She waited.

"Well?" she urged him. "What is the secret?"

After a long, drawn out exhalation he answered, "Something quite unexpected has happened to me."

He made her wait again for the final revelation. She expelled an impatient sigh.

"I have fallen in love," he confessed.

Sarah's face lit up with delight and astonishment.

"My word! I had no idea! You were so indifferent toward Miss Beck when we talked of her before!"

"What makes you think I am referring to Miss Rebecca?"

Sarah looked even more astonished, but considerably less pleased.

"My goodness! You don't mean you fancy Miss Louisa!" she exclaimed. "She is spoken for!"

"No, I don't fancy her, either," the captain assured her.

His sister blinked and quivered in open-mouthed amazement.

"I cannot imagine you would consider anyone so young as Miss Charlotte, so that only leaves Miss Harriott," she marveled.

He smiled broadly and replied, "Yes, Miss Harriott M."

Sarah was speechless for a few moments, then asked, "When did this happen?"

"I couldn't say precisely. I only know that, after spending some time in her company, I found myself thinking of her when not in her company…When I am in her presence, Sarah, I feel so happy and—"

He stopped, catching himself before he revealed any more of his most intimate feelings to his sister.

"Suffice it to say that I am in love with the lady," he concluded.

"Does she know?"

"I think not. Not yet."

"What if she does not return your affections?"

"Then I am a most unfortunate man."

Now it was Sarah's turn to stare off into the distance in a daze.

"Well I never in all my life was so surprised," she murmured.

"Don't you like Miss Harriott?" he asked, unperturbed by her perturbation.

"Why, I love her," Sarah protested, "but I suppose...I suppose I had it set in my mind that she was a spinster, and would always remain so."

"Not if I have my way," he laughed softly.

"When will you tell her?" she asked.

"Soon," he replied, growing serious. "It must be soon."

James reached into a pocket and pulled out a piece of paper. As he opened it, Sarah saw the letterhead of the military department headquarters in Charleston.

"My orders," he said glumly.

CHAPTER SIX

One sunny, very warm afternoon, James walked over to the Briars, arriving a little earlier than he was expected. Mrs. Middleford was out in one of the gardens talking with Wash, and motioned to the captain to go on inside the house. No one greeted him at the door, and he found the parlor deserted except for Harriott, who was sitting at her work table reading. She was so absorbed in her book that she did not realize that Captain Mitchell had come in until he was halfway across the room. Overjoyed to find her alone, he quickly came to her side and asked what she was reading. Harriott showed him the title page of the book.

"A Manual of Domestic Economy," he read aloud, "by Miss Leslie."

"It has a chapter on bee-keeping," she explained. "I am doing so poorly at it, I thought I should consult one of mother's old books to learn more."

She turned back to the page where a section was headed "TO KEEP BEES."

"I have already discovered that I am doing several things wrong," she went on. "You see—"

Harriott pointed to a paragraph and began reading a passage aloud. The captain leaned down, putting his face very close to hers, pretending to read also.

"The hive-benches," she read, "should *not* be placed close to a fence, a tree, or even in the vicinity of tall shrubs or flowers, that they may the less accessible to any thing that is likely to commit depredations on the bees. Ants are their mortal enemies—"

"Mortal enemies!" he echoed, almost in a whisper, and in a strangely lilting, tender tone that seemed to have nothing to do with the subject at hand.

Harriott looked up to find that the captain was gazing at her, and not the book.

"I didn't know that," he said, in much the same tone, and with a look she did not understand, a look that confused and unsettled her as much as his nearness.

"Neither did I," she replied uneasily, abruptly turning her eyes back to her book.

"I hope you are very careful working with the bees," he said gently. "I hate to think of your being stung."

"I am careful."

Harriott closed the book and pushed back the chair a little, and as the captain stood straight again so that she could rise from the table, and was about to speak to her again, all her sisters sauntered into the room and greeted him. Mrs. Middleford came in just afterwards, fanning herself and complaining of the unusual heat. She arranged for some cool apple cider to be served, and the gentleman and the ladies passed an hour in pleasant conversation.

The captain seemed very much at ease as usual as they talked, entertaining the Middlefords with an amusing story about camp life, and Harriott soon forgot her own earlier sense of uneasiness in his presence, and decided she had only imagined that there had been something out of the ordinary in his voice and looks. When it grew uncomfortably warm inside the house, they all went out to the piazza, but found little relief there, as there was no breeze that day.

The girls expressed a desire to cool off somehow, and suddenly settled on the idea of going down to the stream.

"You must come with us, Captain Mitchell," Rebecca insisted. "It's so nice there, and the water is so cool and lovely."

"There is something of a steep walk down to the water," Mrs. Middleford reminded them. "Perhaps the captain would do better on horseback."

"I would like to see the stream," he said.

Harriott also preferred to ride, and went out to the stables to arrange for two horses to be saddled. The girls ran inside to fetch their hats, and Harriott soon reappeared on horseback, leading another horse for Captain Mitchell. These were two older mares, mainly used as carriage horses. One was somewhat swayback, and the other was going blind in one eye, but they were highly prized by the family, and Mrs. Middleford was perpetually anxious for them, fearing they would be stolen like so many horses had been in the area. Two other old horses owned by the family had been put out to pasture before the war, but since then had been called out of retirement for various uses, one old fellow being hired out to a local miller at certain times of the year.

Louisa brought out a hat for Harriott, and as soon as its ribbons were tied, they all set out for the stream. The three sisters walked beside the riders talking incessantly, and within a few minutes, they reached the path through the woods leading to their destination. From here they could already faintly hear the sound of the rushing waters, and in a few more minutes, they were within sight of Briarford Stream, a swiftly moving, rocky creek. They could feel a faint cooling mist rising up to their faces as they made their way down the steep bank to a thin strip of pebbles and sand.

"This is a lovely place," the captain remarked, bringing his horse to a stop on the little beach.

"Isn't it?" said Harriott, whose mare stood close to his. "We spent so many happy hours here as children."

Her sisters sat down on a big sloping rock and began taking off their shoes and stockings.

"You mustn't look at us as we go into water, captain," Rebecca admonished him, hiding her bare feet under her skirt so that even the tips of her toes were covered.

"I shall avert my eyes, ladies," he said with a little laugh. "Are you going to join them, Miss Harriott?"

"Not today."

The girls pulled their skirts up just above the ankles and put their feet into the shallow edges of the stream. The water was icy cold, and it took a few moments for them to get used to it. Gradually, they waded out a little deeper, keeping their hems just above the water level.

"See, Captain Mitchell!" Charlotte called out merrily. "We are not afraid of the water!"

"I see!" he called back. "You are all very brave."

"Don't go out too far, dears," Harriott advised them. "And be careful of the rocks."

The three sisters did move a little farther out into the stream, their objective being a wide flat rock where they wished to sit. Harriott and the captain remained on their horses. As the two riders admired the scenery, and enjoyed the girls' fun, they were quiet, until Captain Mitchell spoke of something that had nothing to do with either.

"I have some news to tell you," he said casually, as if not to elicit any unusual interest.

"Oh?" she responded, matching his casual tone, though very

interested in news of any sort. "Do tell me, then."

"I have received orders to report to Charleston. I am to be promoted to the rank of major, and will be serving on General Beauregard's staff. The army examiners have deemed me unfit for the field of battle because of my injury."

"That disappoints you, I am sure," Harriott observed, feeling real disappointment for his sake, but at the same time, a strange, inexplicable fluttering of happiness, and hopefulness, deep in her heart.

"Yes, it does," he said. "I would willingly return to the fight, but of course I must follow orders, and I must admit, I don't mind the promotion."

"Major Mitchell," she intoned, and he smiled a half-smile proudly at the sound of it.

"When must you go?" she asked after a pause.

"I am to report within two weeks' time."

She nodded and gazed off toward her sisters. When the girls saw that she was watching them, they waved to her and smiled. As Harriott waved back, the captain remarked, "I shall miss Flat Rock very much. I shall miss my sister, who has taken very good care of me, and all my new friends here—one of them more than all the others."

The falling tone of his voice made Harriott look into his eyes, and for a moment she fancied there was an unspoken message there for her, but she quickly corrected herself, thinking that her imagination must be playing tricks on her today, and put away such a notion.

"You mean Turk, of course," she said.

He smiled and shook his head, but she did not interpret this as a denial.

"Will you miss me?" he asked.

"Of course we shall miss you! We have enjoyed your company and friendship very much, and we shall not feel so safe when you are gone."

James gnawed at his mustache, and Harriott knew by now that this was a sure sign of displeasure or irritation. She had learned how to gauge the level of either in him by the amount of mustache that would momentarily disappear into one corner of his mouth. A considerable amount disappeared now, indicating that he was seriously displeased or concerned about something.

"Now you will worry about our safety here in Flat Rock?" she speculated.

He looked off toward the creek, answering after a silence, "Well, there is that, yes. But I wish to tell you…"

He paused, and she waited for the rest.

"I wish to tell you, Miss Harriott, that the person I shall miss most is not your nephew, you see. It is you."

She was too surprised to offer any ready answer.

"I wonder…," he continued, turning to her intently, his eyes full of entreaty, "I wonder if you could possibly entertain feelings deeper than friendship for a lame, ugly man. If you could, this one would like to marry you."

Marry you…

The two words resounded in her ears with the force of a thunderclap, and she saw in his eyes the radiance of an unmistakable tenderness, and knew now that her imagination had not been deceiving her after all.

When she could speak she replied, a little breathlessly, but very carefully, "I certainly regard you as a friend, Captain Mitchell, but more than that, I could not say at this moment. You take me by surprise."

Harriott's mare seemed to sense her agitation, and started

forward a step or two, throwing her head up and down with a snort. The captain caught at the horse's bridle and steadied the animal.

"Will you at least consider the idea of marrying me, before you run away?"

His face relaxed into a smile as he asked the question, and Harriott smiled faintly in return and nodded a 'yes,' going very red in the face. James let go of the bridle, and the horse immediately began moving toward the creek, until her rider directed her to a parallel course. Harriott pretended to be interested in some greenery a little ways downstream, so as not to let her sisters see how flustered she was. After a few minutes, the captain followed after her, bringing his horse to stop beside hers again.

"I might add," he said, in a quiet, earnest way, "in case you have any hesitation about my being a soldier, that with my new orders, my chances of surviving this war have improved considerably...and may I say, that the thought of your companionship for the rest of my life, gives me great hope of happiness in the future, no matter what happens."

No matter what happens. She knew what he meant by that; he meant losing the war, a thought too devastating to bear for long.

"You must give me time," she whispered to him, noting that her sisters were approaching.

He pulled his horse closer.

"At least give me the opportunity to court you, to woo you," he implored. "I am already in love with you, so I have nothing to lose. I have already crossed the Rubicon. Let me see if I can tempt you to do the same."

Harriott opened her eyes very wide with a look meant to silence him, and the captain laughed and beckoned the girls closer. They had paused for some reason, but hurried up to him at this gesture, and it became clear that they had overheard at least a little of the conversation.

"Are you meaning to cross the stream?" Rebecca asked quizzically. "Whatever for?"

"It is too treacherous for crossing on horseback!" Louisa protested.

"A foolish dare!" Charlotte agreed indignantly.

"Only a dare," he laughed, but added with a meaning look to Harriott, "and Miss Harriott may be too wise to take me up on it."

"Of course she is!" said Rebecca. "But you really didn't mean it."

"Oh, Miss Rebecca, you don't know what I meant," the captain sighed lightheartedly.

* * *

Not long after they all returned to the house, Captain Mitchell thanked the ladies for an enjoyable afternoon and started home in his buggy.

Harriott lingered on the piazza and watched him drive away, keeping her eyes on the vehicle as it wound down the hill and disappeared from sight. She was thinking of what he had said about being ordered to Charleston. Projecting herself into the near future, and imagining that his departure now was that final one, she felt an unmistakable heartache, and could not deny it.

"Can it be?" she wondered. "Can it be?"

Wishing to be alone, she told her family that she was a little tired and wanted a nap, and went up to her room. In her bed, she closed her eyes and relived in her mind the startling, momentous event of the day—Captain Mitchell's proposal of marriage. It had thrown her into great agitation and confusion, not only because it was unforeseen, but because of the sudden rush of feelings that it had called up in her—an unexpected blossoming of joy, hope, and longing.

Though she had done her best to conceal these feelings from him, she also began to realize that they must have been hidden in her heart for some time. Harriott knew now that her feelings for James Mitchell were indeed deeper than friendship, but with this knowledge came fear. The country was at war, and he was a soldier. If she let herself love him, and then lost him, she was not sure that she would be strong enough to bear it. The idea of such pain, such loss, stirred up a spirit of denial and self-protection in her.

"I don't love him. I don't," she told herself—all the while knowing it was not true.

* * *

Two days later, when the captain returned to the Briars, hoping that Harriott had by now decided in his favor, and that his visit would develop into a very happy occasion—the announcement of an engagement—he found the Middleford family preoccupied with another visitor. Their cousin Dr. Weston Frost had paid an unexpected call while on furlough.

As the center of attention in the parlor, the young man had been lavished with as many comforts and refreshments as the household could offer, but was having some difficulty enjoying his food and drink, being plied with incessant questions by his relatives. The only interruption allowed was a brief introduction; the captain made the acquaintance of Dr. Frost, an army surgeon, and the interrogations promptly resumed. Turquand was seated on the floor at his cousin's feet, and Gabriel was also close by, his knees resting on an ottoman, his elbows on the arm of the doctor's chair. Both boys were clinging to him and tugging on his clothes now and then for attention.

James took a seat on the periphery of the little circle gathered around the doctor, placing himself directly opposite

Harriott, who had grown quiet and subdued since his arrival. His eyes were already asking her the all-important question again, and seeking an answer, but her expression was neutral and composed, and her eyes gave him no clue.

Later, everyone went outside to enjoy the fine weather and the beauty of the gardens and grounds. Dr. Frost strolled along for a while with Harriott on one arm and Mrs. Middleford on the other, while all the others were scattered around close by. Turquand was telling Gabriel and Captain Mitchell about a hunting adventure of the day before, but the older part of his audience was hardly listening. James had noticed the warm and affectionate looks Harriott gave her cousin as they talked, and was feeling disturbing pangs of jealousy. Dr. Frost was an unmarried man, and not unattractive.

"If only she would look at me that way," he thought, wanting her more than ever now.

While Turquand chattered on, Rebecca and Charlotte passed by strolling arm in arm and, as they did, the captain overheard a snatch of their conversation.

"Oh, yes, but we know who Wes has missed the most," Rebecca was saying in a roguish tone.

"His beloved Louisa!" sighed Charlotte. "Poor Weston! He never gives up."

The rest of what they said died away in giggles and murmurs as they walked on, but James had heard enough to put his jealous fancies to rest. He looked around and noted that Louisa was alone, and had taken a seat on a stone bench under a big oak tree. She looked thoughtful, and was watching her cousin, who frequently turned his head to glance at her.

In the meantime, Harriott was aware that she was being watched. Captain Mitchell had steered the boys in her direction, and was soon at her side. She and her cousin and mother had paused at the edge of one of the flower gardens, where the elder lady was greeting Wash and praising his handiwork. Leaving Dr. Frost and the others, Mrs. Middleford walked over to the old man to converse about matters botanical. Harriott commented that it was rather warm in the sun, and suggested that they view the gardens from a shady spot, so they all walked over to join Louisa under the tree.

Growing bored with adult amusements, the boys began calling for their playmate Josh, who was usually with one or the other at all times. When Harriott told them that she had seen Josh limping that morning, little Gabriel became upset.

"Poor Josh! Won't you help him, Auntie?" he wailed.

"Let's go find him," said Turk.

Captain Mitchell offered to help, and the boys ran off ahead of him. Much to his surprise, Harriott also volunteered her services, and walked with him toward the house.

Sensing that his eyes were questioning her again, she tried to avoid his gaze.

"I am very glad to have a moment alone with you, Miss Harriott," he said.

"Because you are expecting an answer from me," she murmured, looking straight ahead.

"Yes, I am waiting."

"I don't have an answer for you…yet," she said quietly.

"Well, no answer is, I suppose, preferable to the one I don't wish to hear, loving you as I do…but my time here grows short, you know."

"I know that."

Harriott's nephews had coaxed Josh away from a comfortable spot near the piazza and were leading him in her direction. The dog was trying to walk without using one of his front paws, but otherwise did not seem to be in much distress. When they reached her, Harriott leaned over, took the paw in her hand, and diagnosed a thorn, which was quickly removed. Josh whined momentarily with the extraction, but was soon afterwards running about as usual with the boys.

"Well done," the captain commended her.

Harriott smiled slightly and gazed off toward her cousin Weston, who was now seated beside Louisa on the stone bench.

"Is that why you walked with me just now, Miss Harriott?" asked James. "To leave those two alone together?"

She nodded, turning to him with some surprise.

"I overheard your sisters talking of Dr. Frost and Miss Louisa," he explained.

"What did you hear?" asked Harriott.

"That he loves her, though I gather his affections are not returned. Is that correct?"

"That is the case."

"But you obviously wish it were otherwise," he suggested.

"I do," said Harriott, watching Louisa fondly. "I wish it very much."

The captain now contemplated Dr. Frost with a sympathetic pang, hoping not to share the same fate as a lover.

While Harriott and Captain Mitchell conversed, Dr. Frost enjoyed a few moments alone with Louisa. He had walked up to the bench where she sat with a jaunty step, hands in his pockets, and with a wry smile meant to hide his nervousness.

"May I sit with you, Lou?" he asked, pausing and bowing forward a little.

"Of course, Wes," she murmured.

The doctor sat down, necessarily placing himself very close

to her because of the narrowness of the bench, and slapped his hands down on his knees with a great deep breath.

"Ah-h," he breathed out, "this mountain air, this mild climate—so good for one's health."

"Mama calls it champagne air," Louisa remarked.

"And so it is. Are you in good health these days, cousin?"

"I am. Are you, Wes?"

"Surprisingly enough, I am. Though I am surrounded at times by all sorts of maladies and calamities, I seem to thrive. I think it is so much outdoor living—camp life, you know. Physically, I am well, although it is more difficult for me to maintain a healthy frame of mind and spirit."

"Because you see so much suffering?" she guessed.

"Exactly."

Louisa studied him for a few moments and then remarked, "In your letters, I think you do not tell us everything you do and see."

"No, I don't, Lou," he admitted quietly. "I couldn't. The delicate minds and feelings of young ladies ought not to be stained with certain things."

She had no answer for this, and after a silence, Dr. Frost drew in another deep inhalation and gazed around at the beautiful scenery.

"It is so lovely and peaceful here," he observed. "One could almost believe there was no war going on. How I wish all the country were like this place!"

Louisa was about to explain to him about the Tories who troubled this seeming paradise, but quickly thought better of it. Her mother had asked her not to write of such things to Weston and other male friends and relatives. Mrs. Middleford always maintained that men serving the cause ought not to be discouraged by news of troubles at home, and Louisa often wondered if this was reason that their father had not yet moved his family out of Flat Rock.

Mrs. Middleford had left the garden, and was walking toward Louisa and Dr. Frost, followed by Rebecca and Charlotte.

"Is there hope for your cousin?" asked James, as he and Harriott strolled over to join the others in the shade of the hemlock tree.

"Perhaps not now, but someday, I think," she replied.

* * *

Mrs. Middleford insisted that Dr. Frost stay the night with the family at the Briars, and he was glad to do so, though one night was all he could spend in Flat Rock. His parents and sisters were anxious to see him, and he was obliged to leave the next day to visit his family in South Carolina. Like the Middlefords, the Frosts were planters in the Georgetown District, but they also had a home in Charleston, and when both places grew too dangerous, they took refuge with relatives in Camden.

Harriott had noticed from the first how much less awkward and tongue-tied Weston was in Louisa's presence now, but during the family's evening together in the parlor, she watched him carefully, and also saw that in unguarded moments, when he was unaware of any attention in his direction, he sometimes betrayed the same slavish look of adoration for her sister that she remembered in the shy boy of four years past. It was obvious that he loved Louisa as much as ever.

That night, in her bed, while her cousin Weston was in his own bed in the guest room thinking of her, Louisa was thinking of him, and wondering over a subtle but certain change of feeling going on in her heart.

She remembered her cousin Weston as a wiry youth of

nineteen with strawberry blonde hair and a smooth, clean shaven face expressive of gentleness and a certain wistfulness. To her, it was not an unattractive face, yet he had not interested her much as a prospective suitor, and his shyness and awkwardness in her presence had rendered him even less interesting.

Louisa had been surprised when she saw Weston again that day after their long separation. Though still very youthful looking, he had aged to advantage. The creases of maturity around his light blue eyes were pleasing, and the wistfulness in his expression had all but disappeared, replaced with a look of seriousness and confidence. The lower part of his face was smartened by a trim Van Dyke beard of dark red hair, and he had the figure of a man now, solid and well-formed.

Weston had loved Louisa for many years, but she had only loved him as a cousin and friend, and had never before felt a different attraction for him—until now. The letters he had written to her during the war had caused her to realize that there was far more to him than she had ever detected. They had revealed exceptional thoughtfulness, compassion, and humor, as well as the good heart she always knew he possessed, and now, a more pleasing physical appearance had been added to these qualities. So many memories of Weston as a kind of brother, and an awkward youth, were still fresh in her mind, and argued against him, yet Louisa could not deny that she was drawn to him, almost against her will.

CHAPTER SEVEN

Captain Mitchell paid another call to the Briars late the following morning, arriving shortly after Dr. Frost had said his goodbyes to the Middlefords. They all seemed somewhat depressed over his departure. Mrs. Middleford was still dabbing tears away from her eyes with a dainty handkerchief when the captain appeared, but brightened with his greetings and pleasantries. It was another beautiful, balmy day, and he took her for a stroll in the gardens to cheer her and divert her mind.

Later, when James was with all the Middleford ladies again in the parlor, the girls were talking about their brother Arthur and other relations in the army, hoping that furloughs would be granted to these men for visits home. Charlotte asked the captain how much longer he expected to be on leave.

He hesitated with a reluctant, uneasy air, then said, "I've been meaning to tell you ladies something about that."

All three of the younger sisters made sounds and gestures of dismay in unison.

"Oh!" cried Charlotte. "Are you leaving us soon?"

"I'm afraid so. I have received orders to report to Charleston."

He informed them of his staff appointment, and his promotion in rank.

"We must call you Major Mitchell, then," said Mrs. Middleford, smiling ruefully. "No doubt you will be of great service to the cause in Charleston, but we are saddened to lose you."

"Very sad," Louisa agreed.

"We shall miss you very much!" said Charlotte.

Rebecca echoed this sentiment emphatically, but Harriott only murmured a faint "yes" and said nothing more.

"When must you leave us, Captain—or should I say Major?" asked Mrs. Middleford.

"I've only about a week left here," he replied. "And you may still call me captain, as I'll not receive my rank until after I arrive in Charleston."

Turquand and Gabriel had just walked into the room and overheard the bad news. Gabriel rushed over to James and climbed into his lap, and Turquand insisted that they should go fishing everyday while he was still in Flat Rock.

"May I write to you?" asked the boy. "It will be grand to correspond with a major! And will you write to me?"

"We shall all wish to write to you," Louisa added.

"I shall be delighted to have such charming correspondents," he told them graciously.

"The day before you leave," said Mrs. Middleford, "allow us to host a farewell dinner for you, Captain."

"I'd be honored," he replied.

* * *

Hoping that a prolonged absence might possibly make Harriott's heart grow fonder, James did not visit the Briars again until the day of his farewell dinner, and he came alone. His sister had planned to accompany him, but changed her mind when she realized that there was still much to do before she left Flat Rock, and so busied herself packing her belongings and making preparations to close up the house.

The Middlefords had prepared as lavish a meal as possible for the captain, most of the work having been done by the four sisters. Their maid Lilah and the cook were both ill and had taken to their beds.

During the meal Mrs. Middleford did much of the talking, and though her three youngest daughters were saddened by Captain Mitchell's imminent departure, they also took part in the conversation, and tried to make their last day together with him as pleasant as possible. Harriott, on the other hand, hardly uttered a word, ate very little, and smiled only once or twice.

The captain watched her as much as he could without seeming to be preoccupied, wondering what this solemnity and silence meant. He also noticed her lack of appetite, and dared to speculate that she might be lovesick.

"Or perhaps she is depressed that I am leaving," he thought.

If either was the case, he reasoned, then her reserve was a good sign.

Turquand and Gabriel were seated next to each other at the table that afternoon, but eventually had to be separated because of misbehavior. Leaving his chair, Gabriel climbed up into Captain Mitchell's lap and put his arms around his neck.

"We'll miss you, Captain," the boy said mournfully. "I wish I could go to Charleston with you."

"Oh," sighed Rebecca, "we all wish that!"

"It will be so dull here when you are gone," Charlotte complained.

Later, as the meal and conversation drew to an end, the Middleford girls rose and dispersed to clear the table and clean up, but they made Captain Mitchell promise to stay at least another hour or two, and while her daughters worked Mrs. Middleford claimed his company for herself. Making themselves comfortable on the piazza, she and the captain talked of Charleston. She was particular in her request that he write to the family about the goings-on in the city, as they had received almost all their information only from newspapers lately.

Gradually, the old lady grew quieter, listening much more than she talked, and eventually began to look drowsy.

"You must forgive an old woman's weakness," she apologized after a little yawn. "If you don't mind, I think I shall close my eyes for a little while."

"Not at all, Mrs. Middleford," he said. "There is something I wish to discuss with Miss Harriott. Will you excuse me?"

"Certainly, Captain," she murmured, and complacently dozed off as he left her.

He walked into the parlor and thought at first that it was empty, but then saw Harriott at her work table by the window. She was not seated to paint or sketch, but was standing over the table dusting or cleaning it with a rag. She looked up abruptly as the captain approached.

"Gabriel made a spill and quite a mess here just now, I'm afraid," she explained, immediately flustered by his presence.

"I hope it did no harm to your paintings or drawings," he said.

"No harm done, really."

He came to the very edge of the table, facing her.

"I shall be leaving tomorrow, and I wondered…"

Harriott slowly put down the cloth and looked away.

"I wondered if you had any word for me," he concluded.

She stared down at the floor in confusion, not knowing what

to say. Her heart was full of antagonistic emotions, and contradictory answers came into her head.

Seeing that he had caught her at a weak moment, the captain made the most of it.

"Allow me to say again, Miss Harriott, how much I care for you. I adore you! I love you! And I shall be in torment until you say the same to me."

Harriott's confusion was only deepened by these ardent declarations, and her eyes darted toward different parts of the room to avoid meeting his. James moved around the table and drew close to her.

"I should very much like to kiss you before I go," he said.

She looked up, surprised.

"Even though we are not engaged?" she asked, reddening a little.

"Yes, even though we are not engaged. All the indecision is on your part, not mine, you know. May I? If you don't like my kiss, or if you do, it may help you make up your mind."

She stared at him for a few moments, struck by his argument which did not seem quite sound, but which she could not at that moment think how to counter. She was not thinking very clearly.

"Very well," she murmured.

Taking prompt and full advantage of the opportunity, the captain immediately embraced her and pressed to her lips a careful, very skillful kiss. She felt her heart beating in her ears as he slowly and reluctantly released her.

"I love you," he whispered. "Do try to love me, won't you?"

She lowered her head with trembling lips, and when she turned her eyes up to his again, they were full of tears.

"I am trying *not* to love you," she confessed brokenly.

"Why?" he asked, in a strained tone of voice that matched

hers. "What is it that you fear?"

"Can't you guess?"

He sighed heavily.

"Dear, I shall be in far less danger than I have ever been in this war, don't you understand that?"

"When your leg is well again, you will go back to the fight. I know you will."

"I'm pretty certain that my leg will never be completely well again. But my girl, what kind of a man would I be if I did not go back to the fight when capable of doing so?"

"You see? I am right! I know you."

He studied her tearful, earnest expression, and a smile slowly lifted the corners of his mustache.

"Miss Harriott, I shall write you such love letters that you will not be able to resist me," he said. "Then I shall request a furlough to come up here and marry you."

She smiled and even laughed a little in spite of herself.

"How impertinent you are," she sniffed.

He made no answer, but looked into her eyes so lovingly that she felt all her defenses crumbling.

"I must be leaving very soon now," he reminded her.

Harriott bit her lip, struggling against him with the last remnants of her strength, then suddenly shook her head and threw her arms around his neck.

"Oh, why do I torture the both of us?" she cried. "I will marry you, Captain Mitchell, and I believe I do love you."

"Ah," he sighed, enfolding her tightly. "That is what I wished to hear."

A moment later, several jaws dropped as Harriott's sisters entered the parlor and saw the captain embracing her.

"Harrie!" Rebecca cried, nearly shrieking.

Harriott wiped away tears of happiness from her eyes and announced that she was engaged to be married to Captain Mitchell.

Her sisters stared, still open-mouthed, but Rebecca managed to stammer, "We—we had no idea! This comes as a great surprise. Why didn't you tell us, Harrie?"

"Captain Mitchell proposed to me last week, but I have only just now accepted him," she explained.

"You ought to have told us last week!" Charlotte protested.

"Oh, don't be silly, girls," Louisa interposed. "Harrie had her reasons! I for one am very happy for you both. Let me be the first to congratulate you."

She rushed over to embrace Harriott, and the other two did likewise, showing their happiness for her effusively with exclamations, sighs, and laughter.

"And we are very happy for you, Captain Mitchell," said Rebecca, turning to him. "We shall be so glad to call you our brother."

He thanked them all warmly, but all the while, could hardly take his eyes off Harriott, as he basked in the affection and attachment toward him that was now evident and openly expressed in her looks and her whole being. She gravitated close to him and took his hand as her sisters continued with all kinds of exclamations and questions. One of those questions gave the captain pause.

"Does Mama know of your engagement?" Louisa asked curiously.

James turned to Harriott with a sudden look of concern.

"You know," he said, "I ought to have approached your mother for her permission, or written to your father first, but when I received my orders for Charleston, I felt I had so little time. I suppose all that went out of my head— until now."

"You could speak to Mama now," Harriott suggested.

Her sisters nodded eagerly and pointed toward the piazza to encourage him. With a broad smile, and eyebrows raised very high, but with some nervousness, he left the parlor and walked out to the piazza alone, finding Mrs. Middleford still in her favorite chair, and now wide awake.

"Where are the girls?" she asked, surprised. "They went to find you."

"They found me," he replied. "May I have a private word with you, Mrs. Middleford?"

"Certainly, Captain."

Feeling awkward on his feet, he pulled up a chair to face hers and sat down.

"Mrs. Middleford," he began, clearing his throat as he contemplated what to say next. "I think I shall be direct with you. I wish to marry one of your daughters."

The old lady smiled slowly and asked, "Have you decided which one?"

He laughed, and she joined him, looking very pleased.

"Miss Harriott," he replied.

Mrs. Middleford did not seem surprised at his choice.

"I have observed the friendship which has blossomed between the two of you," she said quietly. "I could tell that Harrie was very fond of you, though she endeavored not to show it too much."

"I love her very much. I ought to have come to you first, but when I received my orders for Charleston, I wished to waste no time in making my feelings known to her."

"Well, these are unusual times, Captain, and Harriott is not a young girl whose judgment might be questioned. I take it she has accepted your proposal."

"After some consideration, yes, I am happy to say."

"Then you certainly have my blessing, Captain Mitchell. I shall write to my husband directly and state your case for you. He will be reluctant to part with Harriott, as am I, but I am sure he will put no obstacles in the way of her happiness."

"Thank you, Mrs. Middleford," he said gratefully, with a sigh of relief.

Harriott's mother smiled on him again benignly and remarked, "You have got yourself a treasure, Captain."

"Well I know it, Mrs. Middleford," he replied. "Well I know it."

* * *

When the captain returned to the parlor, his smile told Harriott and her sisters all they needed to know, but he briefly reported what their mother had said, and then, suddenly, took on an odd, contrite look, and told them that he had a confession to make.

"I told you that I was leaving tomorrow," he said sheepishly, "but I reserved one extra day in case Miss Harriott accepted my proposal, and so you see I really have one more day—tomorrow—before I must go. I hope you will all forgive me this little deception."

"And what if Harrie had not accepted your proposal?" asked Louisa.

"Well then, I would have made this my last day here in Flat Rock."

"In that case I don't think there was really any deception," Louisa declared. "Obviously you did not expect the answer you received today."

"I don't suppose I did," he replied, taking Harriott's hand. "But I'm very glad for it."

They all walked out to the piazza to join Mrs. Middleford. The newly engaged couple stood arm in arm facing her, and the girls clustered around their mother in the chairs. Everyone was happy and talkative, and Harriott's sisters began entertaining themselves by speculating about wedding plans, and a wedding dress. Mrs. Middleford had preserved her late daughter's wedding dress, a beautiful gown of white satin, and thought it would just fit Harriott, but it was packed away in a trunk in South Carolina, and she wondered if it would be possible for her husband to send it to Flat Rock.

"I don't see why not, Mama," Louisa opined. "But he must be careful to pack the dress well, in something light, so that no one will think it is food or something else valuable and be tempted to take it."

"I shall write to him about the matter," said Mrs. Middleford. "We might as well have it with us."

"Oh, but what if the dress is lost?" Charlotte fretted. "Where shall we find another?"

"I suppose it is a risk we must take," her mother replied resignedly.

While the others continued to talk about the wedding, James leaned closer to Harriott and spoke in her ear in a whisper.

"I have so little time with you before I must leave, and I should very much like to have you to myself at least a little while. Might we go and sit on that bench near the big hemlock tree?"

The bench he spoke of was in plain sight of anyone on the piazza, but far enough away to ensure that conversation from that quarter would not be overheard. Harriott answered by tugging at his arm and moving toward the front steps. Her mother's face registered some surprise.

"Mama," Harriott said to her over her shoulder, "if you will excuse us, the day is so lovely, Captain Mitchell and I shall take a walk now."

Louisa, Rebecca, and Charlotte suddenly fell silent and watched their sister descend the steps and stroll away arm in arm with her fiancé. After a leisurely turn around the yard, the two sat down on the bench, their backs to the piazza.

"Are we being observed?" the captain asked facetiously.

"Of course we are," said Harriott. "And Mama will certainly not leave the piazza until I return."

"Well, at least we have the privacy of some distance. Now that we are engaged, there are many things I have to say that are for your ears only. First, I wish to tell you how much I love you, and value your love. You do love me, don't you? You were not quite positive about that before."

"I am positive that I love you," she said, with some difficulty.

"I don't think it is easy for you to say. Why is that?" he wondered.

"Perhaps...because...everything is so uncertain these days."

"Ah, that again," he sighed. "But darling, even if there were no war, life would still be uncertain. You are wise enough to know that."

"I can't help it. I shall be afraid for you, as I have been afraid for my brother, and others. I can't help it, but I will bear it—I must."

"That's my girl," he praised her, squeezing her hand.

She rested her head against his shoulder and took a deep, contented breath.

"Are you happy?" he asked.

"I am."

"So am I."

Curious about Sarah's feelings on their engagement, Harriott asked James if he had told his sister of his feelings for her.

"I did," he said, then looked reminiscent, and chuckled.

"Why do you laugh?" she asked.

"When I first told her that I had fallen in love, she jumped to the conclusion that the lady was your sister Rebecca."

"Really!" Harriott marveled, though only momentarily. "But why am I surprised? Beck is beautiful and of marriageable age."

"My sister then assumed that I fancied Miss Louisa, and was quite scandalized."

"I suppose it is natural she would think of those two first. They are both beautiful young ladies. Now I am wondering why you did not fall in love with one of them."

"I found you far more interesting and charming—not to disparage your sisters."

"Oh, they are young, that's all. There is more to them than what you have seen, especially Louisa. Two years ago, a young man who had been in love with her for several years finally obtained his father's permission to marry, and asked Lou. She cared for him, but did not accept him at first. They corresponded many months, while he was in the army in Virginia, and at last she made up her mind that she would marry him, but the next letter she received from him was written from a hospital in Richmond, and not long afterwards, we learned that he had died of his wounds."

"Very sad," said the captain.

"Yes…Lou was so deeply grieved, and so very regretful that she had not married him when he wished. Since his death, she seems to have closed up her heart. Our cousin Dr. Frost loves her madly, and writes to her every week, but she told me months ago that she had determined to regard him only as a kinsman and a friend, nothing more."

"Poor fellow. I liked him very much."

"He is such a fine man, kind and devout, but before the war, I'm afraid Louisa was too young to appreciate him. She thought him rather dull. He is quiet, and a bit shy, but I should never call him dull. His letters have been very interesting, and I think they have caused Lou to modify her opinions about him a bit, but she still won't permit him to write to her of love."

"But you said there might be hope for him in the future."

"It's possible, and I don't think she could do better..."

James expressed his sympathies for the lovelorn cousin again, and afterwards, they sat in silence for a while enjoying the luxury of each other's nearness. The late afternoon light began to soften into twilight, as the ruddy glow of the western sky slowly darkened.

"I like this time of day, don't you?" asked Harriott.

"I do. I always have," he answered. "And it is even more pleasant in your company. I shall miss these cool, lovely evenings in the mountains—the trees, the views—but most of all, I shall miss my Harriott M."

She raised her head and looked at James curiously.

"Why do you say my name that way?" she wanted to know.

He hesitated, but could not hide a smile, which made her even more curious.

"What is so amusing?" she asked.

"Harriott M. is how you signed your letter, the one my sister returned to you."

"Yes, she said that she saw my name written thus, as the letter had been torn open."

"That's not all she saw."

"Do you mean to say that she read the letter?"

"A small part of it, and she read that part aloud to me," he said contritely, "about your birthday."

"Oh—h."

Harriott's expression fluctuated between irritation and embarrassment.

"It was wrong of her," he apologized. "I told her not to read it."

"But she did read it," said Harriott, "and you listened."

"I did," he admitted. "Will you forgive me?"

He looked so sincerely sorry that she could not help but pardon him. She gave a sudden laugh and shook her head.

"I don't suppose there was any great harm in it, although it is a little disconcerting to think that you knew some of my innermost thoughts, before we even met."

"Harriott, the few lines my sister read to me, only made me think well of you and, once I met you, and came to know you better …well, you know what that led to."

"You fell in love?"

"I fell in love with Harriott M," he said, and, risking displeasure on the piazza, he put his arm around her and drew her closer for a kiss.

CHAPTER EIGHT

Late the next morning, Captain Mitchell returned to the Briars for a final visit. Sarah was with him, and on first sight of Harriott, she rushed over and embraced her.

"I am so happy for you both!" she cried, beaming affectionately at her future sister-in-law. "I could not ask for a better sister."

For much of the day the engaged couple was the center of attention in the household, but since it was Captain Mitchell's last day among them, the Middlefords eventually centered their attention on him and claimed his company, taking him away from Harriott while the rest of the family, including the two boys, walked with him in the gardens.

Sarah, who was feeling tired out from all the work and concerns of the previous day, sat with Harriott on the piazza, and they talked and watched the others strolling whenever they were in sight. Harriott was curious to know more about the family into which she was marrying, and after a while brought the conversation around to that subject. When Sarah repeated how happy she was about the engagement, Harriott saw her opportunity.

"I'm very glad we have your blessing," she said. "I hope your mother will also approve."

"James has already written to her about you," Sarah confided, leaning closer. "He says she is not displeased, far from it. She says that if his descriptions of you are to be believed, that he is the most fortunate man in the world!"

Amused, Harriott remarked, "Your mother sounds like a very sensible woman."

"Oh, she is, and I agree with her. My brother is very fortunate to have your affections. It's so good to see him happy again—I don't think I have seen James like this for a number of years."

"Has he had so much unhappiness?" Harriott asked sympathetically.

Sarah considered her answer carefully before she began slowly, "He has. He has seen many of his fondest hopes…thwarted, or taken from him. What I mean is, our father, who passed away before the war began, ruled over him very firmly, and wished to mold him in a certain way, and it frequently brought him unhappiness. I don't mean to say that our father was a cruel man— he was not—but he was stern and exacting with his children, especially his only son. Just after James was graduated from college, he wished to marry a young lady he had met in Columbia, but father forbade the match, and James reluctantly gave her up. He was very young, of course, and she was only sixteen or seventeen, and I really think it may have been for the best."

She paused, then went on, "My father also prevailed when it came to my brother's profession. James had a propensity and a love for architecture and art, but was allowed to pursue neither course very far. My father allowed him to take an extended grand tour in Europe, and to indulge those propensities for a while, but when he came home to Charleston, he was expected to follow the path that had been laid out for him, to join father in his business, and so, accordingly, he did."

"Your father was a merchant, I believe? I have heard of the firm of Mitchell and Son."

"Oh yes, he was a most prosperous factor. James worked hard to please father, and the only time he went against his wishes was his choice of a wife, but unfortunately that happiness was short lived, for they had only been married three years when she died with their first child, a stillborn boy. After her death, James found solace in his art, and began to paint again."

"That was five years ago," said Harriott.

"Yes, it's almost five years now. Our father passed away after a long illness not so very long after my brother lost his young wife, but before he died, he called James to him and asked his forgiveness. He said he had ruled over him too much, and regretted it now. My mother worshipped our father, but in the end, even she acknowledged that he had cause to ask his son's pardon."

"What sort of person is your mother?" Harriott wondered.

"Mama," said Sarah, "is a proud, rather undemonstrative lady. Unlike me she is not a very talkative person. Though she does not always show her feelings, they run deep, a fact that is sometimes evident in an outburst of fiery temper every now and then."

"I hope she will like me," said Harriott, looking a little concerned.

"Dear, don't worry. I know Mama will love you," Sarah reassured her. "Don't imagine she will be jealous of you. She is not that sort of person. She will be glad that her son has found a good wife."

They heard talking and laughter from the yard, and turned

to see Captain Mitchell approaching with Turquand and Gabriel.

"How happy he looks," Sarah observed. "And look how James walks, as if he hardly needed the cane now!"

"He is walking much better now," Harriott agreed.

"He says you are good for him," Sarah added, "like a tonic for body and soul."

Having said their final farewells, the boys ran off, and Captain Mitchell joined the ladies on the piazza.

"I've exacted solemn promises of good behavior from your nephew Turk," he announced, taking a chair next to Harriott.

She smiled skeptically. "Have you now? We'll see about those."

"Yes," he laughed, "you must let me know how quickly they are broken."

"Where are the ladies?" Sarah asked her brother.

"Oh, they went to see about the sick servants," he replied. "They will be with us directly, they said."

He flashed his sister a meaning look with his answer, and she understood.

"Will you excuse me?" she said, getting up from her chair. "I find I am quite thirsty, and shall see about getting something to drink. May I bring you something?"

Pretending to believe this story, Harriott and James declined her offer and readily excused her.

While they were alone together, they talked about a wedding date, a matter which had not yet been settled. Though they both wished to marry sooner, it was decided that a spring wedding would be best, possibly in the month of May. The captain hoped that his injured leg would be fully healed by then, and if not, that the milder weather of that season would make for easier travel to the mountains. He told Harriott that his sister had offered her summer house in Flat Rock for their honeymoon.

"I've grown to love this place," he went on, "and it would be a most beautiful setting for our wedding, but I wish you and your family would return to South Carolina. I fear things will only grow worse here for you."

"I have told you of our relations living in Greenville," said Harriott. "My cousin Miss Mary McCord has been anxious for us to come there for some time, and our uncle, Mr. Singleton, who is a lawyer there, told us that he can find a place in town for all of us."

"I would feel much less anxious for you, dear, if you were in Greenville. And how much easier and quicker it will be for me to visit you on furlough! I wish…"

He leaned closer to her, as if about to kiss her.

"I wish your mother would make up her mind to take you all back to South Carolina now. Perhaps we could marry sooner, if there was not so much distance and difficult terrain between us."

Harriott also leaned forward, and a kiss was completed.

"I wish it, too," she whispered. "Whatever brings me closer to you, that is what I wish for."

James took his fiancée's hand, kissed it, and gazed at her contentedly.

"I'm in such a good mood this evening," he said, "but I shall be miserable tomorrow."

"I hope the journey will not be too uncomfortable for you," said Harriott. "You have made such a good recovery, I hope it will cause you no harm."

"I'll be fine, dear."

She reached over to a little table beside her chair and picked up two small pillows covered in homespun cloth.

"I've made these for you. The coach and cars can give one such a jarring, jolting ride sometimes, I thought they might cushion and protect your injured leg, if you rested your foot on one pillow, and put the other under your knee."

"How thoughtful of you, Harriott!"

James took the little pillows and placed them just as she had suggested.

"That's very comfortable," he remarked, and thanked her. "Now don't worry about me, my dear. I shall write to you as soon as I reach Charleston."

* * *

The first letter Harriott received from her fiancé was dated even before his arrival in Charleston. While stopping over in the capital city of Columbia in the mid-state, he sent off a message to let her know that his travels had so far not affected his leg adversely, that he already missed her terribly, and that he would write to her again as soon as he reached his destination.

He kept his word, and the next letter she received from him was dated two days after the first one, from Charleston. Captain Mitchell, he reported, was now Major Mitchell, and was quartered with General Beauregard and the rest of his staff in a fine hotel.

"I share a room," he wrote, "with a Captain Henry Wyatt, whom you would find most interesting. He is an Englishman, formerly of the British Army, who ran the blockade last year to enlist in our army. He is very intelligent and pleasant, and a very good officer. Some months ago, General Beauregard commissioned him and a few others to compile a documentary history of the siege of Charleston. This is only one of the captain's duties, of course, and he has fought in several engagements in this area over the past year. He has many interesting stories to tell of his days in India and China, and I think he will be good company for me, especially in the evenings, when I am more at the mercy of leisure, and therefore more liable to be subject to the blues, thinking of you so far away, my dear Harriott. The Yankees have not shelled the city again since the initial bombardment in August, but it is expected they will begin again before long. More residents have fled the city since that time. I visited my house on Broad Street (the Department's headquarters are also on Broad) and found it in good order. Old Stephen, my father's valet, is well, and goes to the house nearly every day to take care of things there."

* * *

In October, on a sunny, unseasonably warm day, a detachment of mounted riflemen from South Carolina was passing through the Flat Rock area, and stopped to encamp near the Briars. Two of their officers came to the driveway gate, where Jeffrey, the gardener's youngest son, happened to be working on some repairs that afternoon. After introducing themselves and inquiring about the owner of the property, they asked for food, and the young man ran up to the house to relay their request to Mrs. Middleford.

"South Carolinians, you say? Were they well-mannered men?" she inquired.

"Yes'm," Jeffrey replied, looking impatient. "They was polite enough."

"Then go and tell them they may come up to the house," she instructed him.

Jeffrey was already turning to go, though headed in the wrong direction.

"Where are you going?" she asked him.

"I'm gone hide the horses," he said. "Folks says soldiers is impressin' horses for the army!"

"Not these soldiers, surely. Go and give them my message."

Jeffrey sighed resignedly, shook his head with a look prophesying certain regret to come, and loped off down the driveway muttering something under his breath. In a few minutes,

Mrs. Middleford saw two uniformed men walking up the carriage drive. One was a middle-aged gentleman, a captain in rank, and the other, a lieutenant, was a slender young man, likely still in his teens, she guessed. Their uniforms were old and weather beaten, and their faces were covered with the grime of several days' riding on dry, dusty roads. She found them polite, as Jeffrey had described them, and learned that they were reserve troops, a small group on their way to Warm Springs, numbering less than fifty men. The captain was apologetic about his request for food.

"I'm sure you haven't much to spare," he said, "but whatever you can spare, will be greatly appreciated by my men."

Feeling well-disposed toward fellow South Carolinians, Mrs. Middleford told him she would do what she could for them. She suggested that they encamp on the grounds of the Briars, pointing out a pleasant part of the yard near the kitchen house.

The captain's weary face lit up with a smile, and he thanked her profusely, beaming with even greater happiness when he learned that there was a stream on the property where his men could bathe.

"You won't mind our campfires, I hope," he said, and as he and Mrs. Middleford continued to talk, Charlotte came out to the piazza, surprised to see her mother conversing with soldiers. She could see the captain, who stood facing her, and when he tipped his hat and bowed, the young lieutenant turned and looked up at her. He had just lifted his hat to mop a damp handkerchief across his brow, revealing a swath of clean, fair skin, but, dirty as he was, she could tell that he was a young man of extraordinary good looks. His striking, pale blue eyes seemed to glow like two blue lights from his grayish, dust covered face.

While Charlotte stared at him, transfixed, the lieutenant bowed to her, also keeping his eyes fixed on hers, though he had to look away when his captain addressed him.

"Come, Wilson," he said, patting the young man on the shoulder. "Let's go get the men."

Charlotte immediately glided down the steps and to her mother's side.

"Mama, are soldiers coming here?" she asked.

"Captain Boyle's men will camp near the house," replied Mrs. Middleford, who then introduced her youngest to the officers.

"I have a daughter about your age," said the captain, smiling on her wistfully. "And nearly as pretty as you are."

Charlotte smiled and blushed, but not because of the compliment. She was flushed with the infatuation that had taken hold of her, the same infatuation evident in the young lieutenant, though he tried to conceal it. As he followed his captain down the carriage drive, he looked back at Charlotte several times.

Mrs. Middleford went back into the house to announce that guests were imminent, and to order the preparation of food for them. Charlotte meanwhile returned to the piazza and waited, hearing from inside the excited voices and movements of her sisters. Soon Louisa and Rebecca joined her, just in time to see the mounted soldiers coming into sight at the farthest curve of the sloping drive. About a dozen black men were riding with them, a few leading pack mules.

Seeing pretty girls, the younger soldiers raised their hats high in greeting, and some twirled them about in the air. Enthusiastic whoops rose up out of several parched, dusty throats, but the captain quickly checked any further expressions of masculine jubilation with a gesture and a brisk reprimand.

Charlotte kept her eyes on the handsome lieutenant, who rode beside the captain at the front of the column. Likewise his eyes again were on her, and he bowed his head in her direction as they passed by and then disappeared from view around the side of the house. At the rear of the column, one grinning, comical young private leaned back on his horse in order to keep the girls in sight as long as possible. When fully horizontal, he nearly toppled off his saddle, eliciting laughter and hoots from his companions.

The three sisters rushed into the house and went to the window that looked out on the part of the yard where the soldiers were to encamp. Harriott and her mother were soon beside them.

"I invited the officers to come inside," said Mrs. Middleford. "But they said they were too unpresentable."

"They do look in need of a washing," Louisa remarked.

"I told the captain about our stream, and I think they intend to make use of it."

"Oh, Mama, how shall we feed so many?" Rebecca fretted.

Mrs. Middleford reminded her of the fifty bushels of corn which had just been purchased (at the very high price of nearly fifty gold dollars). There was also some salt beef she was willing to give them, along with dozens of eggs. The family table would suffer for these offerings, but the Middlefords had never hesitated to make reasonable sacrifices for the army.

When she was alone in the parlor, Charlotte walked about like one in a trance, going from one window to another to see if she could catch another glimpse of the young man who had fascinated her. Not seeing him from any of these points, she went out to the piazza, working up the courage to go to the part of the porch that wrapped around the corner of the house, where she would be exposed to the view of the soldiers' encampment. Having been informed of the nearby stream by their captain, many were walking in that direction to bathe, while their servants saw to the care of the horses.

Charlotte pulled up a chair and waited for more than an

hour, until she saw the men returning, now considerably cleaner and in high spirits, talking, laughing, and jostling each other as they meandered back to their camp. In a little while, Lilah and another female servant emerged from the kitchen with food, which was received with hearty cheers.

After everyone had eaten, the black men headed for the stream to take their turn at washing, carrying some laundry with them also, and many of the soldiers spread blankets under the trees and lay down to rest. It happened that the young officer Charlotte hoped to see soon seated himself on the ground with his back against a tree, facing in her direction, and it was not long before he spied her on the piazza. The lieutenant stared at her, and she did not look away, but gazed at him steadily in return. He was the first to look away. He glanced around at his fellow soldiers, all of whom were absorbed in letter writing, reading, or sleep, and then slowly rose to his feet. He moved toward the house, but after a few steps he stopped and waited to see if Charlotte would be alarmed or offended by his approach. Seeing that she did not move, he continued in her direction, and walked right up to the piazza.

He was not smiling—she had noticed that he seldom smiled—but he thanked her for her family's hospitality, and for the food, in a polite, pleasant way.

"We are happy to help our soldiers in any way that we can," she replied.

His face, now clean and refreshed, was one of the handsomest she had ever seen. His dark brown hair was wet, but combed to neatness except for a few strands that fell over one side of his forehead. The remarkable blue eyes, framed by thick black lashes and fine eyebrows, mesmerized Charlotte so much that she had to force herself to look away from him time to time as they conversed.

He admired the beauty of Flat Rock, and was asking her many questions about the area—but while the two young people communicated with words, a deeper, much more significant conversation was going on between them.

They talked of his family, and hers. He had two older brothers in the army, in Virginia, and his father was the rector of a church in Columbia, South Carolina. Charlotte had cousins there, and wondered if he knew them. They discovered a few mutual acquaintances.

At one point, he turned and glanced back at his comrades, some of whom were observing him and Charlotte, remarks, smiles, and nudges passing among them as they watched. The handsome young officer turned back to her with an apologetic look.

Before he could speak again she asked, "Will you be leaving us very early in the morning?"

"Most likely," he answered, with obvious regret.

Charlotte worked up the daring to say, "I wish you could stay with us longer."

"So do I," he said, and, emboldened by her boldness, he made a request.

"I wonder if I may write to you, Miss Middleford."

Her answer was prompt.

"You may."

"Your mother will not think it improper of me, I hope."

"I think not," said Charlotte, though she was not entirely sure that her mother would approve. Then she remembered that the young man was the son of a clergyman, and convinced herself that this fact would assuage any maternal objections.

When she gave the lieutenant this assurance, he smiled, and though the smile made him look more boyish, it had as powerful effect on her as an outright profession of love, and she could not help but return it.

After a few parting words, he backed away and paused, smiled again, and reluctantly went back to his camp.

CHAPTER NINE

That night, after everyone inside and outside the house was asleep or at least in bed, Charlotte wrapped herself in a robe and a shawl and tiptoed down the stairs. There was such bright moonlight glowing through the windows that a candle was unnecessary.

She unbolted the door as quietly as possible and stepped out to the piazza, where a cool, brisk breeze swept over her face. The trees and shrubbery were rustling in the moving air, and everything was starkly defined in shades of black and gray by the moonlight and the dark shadows it cast.

Charlotte moved slowly to the far end of the piazza, to the corner where she had talked with her soldier earlier. Reaching out to catch the arm of the chair, a nearby sound startled her as she sat down.

She heard her name spoken in a whisper, and recognized the voice.

"Miss Middleford?"

"Is that you, Lieutenant Wilson?"

"It is!"

He moved out of the deep shadow of a tree, and she saw him clearly, standing in the very spot where he had stood earlier that day.

"My prayers have been answered," he said, keeping his voice low. "I am astonished, but it is true! You are here."

"You have been praying?" she asked.

"For this very thing, yes—as unlikely, no, nearly impossible as it seemed, I did. Why—why did you come out here tonight?"

"You know why," she whispered after a pause. "I wasn't praying, only hoping. I could not sleep."

The young man took hold of the wooden porch railing, propelled himself upward with an acrobatic swing, and perched himself on the very edge of the floorboards. He kept behind the railing, but leaned over it to be closer to her.

"Miss Middleford—may I call you Miss Charlotte?"

"You may."

"Miss Charlotte, I must tell you something, and do forgive me if I offend you. I am in love with you!"

"You do not offend me," she murmured, lowering her eyes shyly.

"Since I first saw you, I think of only you. Is it possible? Is it? We are both so very young. My name is Christopher. I am eighteen, and shall be nineteen next month. How old are you?"

"Sixteen."

"Sixteen," he repeated dreamily. "So very young! How pretty you are in the moonlight, like an angel. You must have thought I was a ghost when I spoke to you out of the darkness."

"No! I didn't think that," she said uneasily. "Please, don't speak of ghosts."

"I don't wish to speak of anything that displeases you, Miss Charlotte."

The chilly breeze gusted more strongly, and she shivered a little.

"You mustn't stay out here much longer," he said. "You might take a cold. It is enough for me that I have seen you again, and said to you what I had to say."

He looked at her expectantly.

"I think of only you—too," she confessed.

A fear suddenly seized her that one of the soldiers, or one of her family, might discover her on the piazza with her lover, and she stood to her feet, pulling the shawl around her more tightly, now trembling nervously.

"You will write to me?" she asked.

"Very soon! And as often as you will permit me."

"I shall pray for your safety, and success."

"If an angel is praying for me, I shall have both."

Charlotte knew she had to leave him now, but it was hard to resist the magnetism that attracted her in the opposite direction. Lieutenant Wilson held out his hand to her. She hesitated, but put out her hand and let him hold it for a few moments.

"Good night, Miss Charlotte," he said. "I hope you will sleep tonight. I think I'll be able to sleep now."

She said good night, and he let go of her hand, but touched it again before it was withdrawn, caressing it softness with his fingertips.

He waited until she made her way to the door and disappeared inside, and then jumped down from the porch to return to his blanket.

The next morning, the Middleford ladies went out to talk to the soldiers as they breakfasted. The men were respectful and well-behaved, and Charlotte took the opportunity to converse with Lieutenant Wilson as much as she could, though under her mother's watchful eye. When it was time for the men to leave, the ladies returned to the piazza, waving to the men as they rode away. The lieutenant turned in his saddle and looked back at Charlotte until the trees along the drive obscured their view of each other. She had to crush down an impulse to run after him, and as soon as she did, she burst into tears and ran into the house.

"What is the meaning of that?" her mother wondered aloud.

The three sisters looked one to the other, and Harriott replied, "I'm sure she is thinking of their going into danger, Mama. Such fine young men…"

"Ah, yes," said Mrs. Middleford, nodding gravely. "It is very sad our young men must shoulder such burdens, and face so many dangers."

"They were very grateful for our hospitality," Rebecca observed more cheerily. "And weren't they polite and gentlemanly? Such officers and soldiers make me proud."

A little while later, Harriott went up to Charlotte's room and found her curled up in her bed. She was no longer weeping, but she looked miserable.

"Lottie," she said softly, taking a seat beside her. "What is the matter, dear?"

Charlotte pouted, "If I tell you, you will laugh at me."

"I will not. I promise."

After a long silence, Charlotte told her sister that she was in love.

"With the handsome lieutenant," Harriott calmly suggested.

"Yes. And he is in love with me, Harrie. He told me so."

Harriott's eyes widened at this revelation.

"There was nothing improper!" Charlotte quickly assured her, sitting up. "He would not have spoken so to me, if I had not—"

She stopped, realizing that what she was about to say would sound very improper.

"He asked my permission to write to me," she went on. "And

I gave it to him. He is the son of a clergyman, and he told me that I looked like an angel."

Harriott's eyes traveled round in rumination for a few moments, but then she sighed, smiled ruefully and said, "I suppose there is no harm in his writing to you, Lottie. But if Mama objects, it must stop."

"Do you think she will object?"

"I don't know, perhaps. She will wish to read his letter, and if it is acceptable, perhaps she'll allow it."

"Oh, I know it will be acceptable," sighed Charlotte, smiling a little now. "Oh, Harrie, don't you think he is the most beautiful young man you ever saw?"

"He's very handsome, but you are both very young."

Charlotte drew herself up to a very straight, dignified posture and, looking at her older sister with all the gravity and determination that her sixteen year-old face could express, she declared, "I love him, and someday, we shall marry."

Harriott suppressed a smile, but half-believed her.

* * *

As the weeks went by, the letters from Major Mitchell in Charleston were a regular but much anticipated occurrence for Harriott as well as the whole family. Though there were many personal sentiments in them that she kept to herself, she would often read aloud the parts relating any interesting news of the goings-on in the city and its environs. The first letter from Lieutenant Wilson arrived about two weeks after his departure, and Mrs. Mitchell insisted on reading it before she allowed Charlotte to do so. She was so pleased, however, with the intelligence, education, and gentility evident in the writer, that she eventually allowed her daughter to conduct a private correspondence with the young man.

In early November, James wrote of meeting a very famous personage. The president of the Confederacy, Jefferson Davis, paid a visit to Charleston, and General Beauregard and staff had taken him to inspect some of the troops on nearby James Island.

"It was quite a day for us all," the major wrote. "The President was stately but most gracious, and the men were on their best behavior. They cheered him heartily, and made a good showing, ill fed and ill clad though many of them were—coatless, and worse. President Davis stopped to speak with a young private, and, noticing his bare feet, asked him where his shoes were. 'By god,' said the boy, 'I ain't got none.'"

Later that month, one of Major Mitchell's letters reported that the enemy had begun throwing shells into Charleston again from Morris Island. By the end of the year, it had become too dangerous to remain in the lower part of the peninsula, and General Beauregard moved his headquarters from Broad Street to a large house in the upper section of the city.

In Flat Rock, the winter passed somewhat uneventfully for the Middlefords, though many rumors of continued Tory outrages in the region reached them, as well as depressing news of military setbacks throughout the Confederacy. Food supplies, most importantly corn, grew scarce, especially after soldiers passing through consumed considerable amounts of that staple.

On the first day of April 1864, the residents of Flat Rock were in a state of unusual agitation as a large number of Confederate troops moved through the area. That morning, a neighbor had sent a note to the Middlefords warning them to hide their horses and corn. These troops, said the message, were "Armstrong's dreaded division," reportedly consisting of regiments from Texas, Arkansas, and Tennessee, who were known to be rather indiscriminate in their foraging. Mrs. Middleford's servants locked all the livestock inside the stables and hid several bushels of corn inside an upstairs bedroom.

Several young officers from this division rode up to the Briars in the afternoon, asked for food and music, and conducted themselves politely, but about an hour after they left, another group of about a dozen men arrived, only one of whom was an officer. Spying these horsemen from a front window, Mrs. Middleford sent her youngest daughters to their rooms. She called Harriott to her side, and the two women stepped out to the piazza arm in arm.

The soldiers rode up to within a few feet of the house and halted, while Harriott and her mother looked the group over with some dismay.

They were gaunt, bearded, rustic-looking men obviously roughened by many battles and hardships. Silent and unsmiling, they offered no greetings or courtesies to the ladies. It was a cold, windy day, and though she was a little afraid of these men, Harriott felt pity for them when she saw that many were without overcoats or shoes. Only about half were attired in any semblance of a uniform, and some were wearing boots, coats, and accoutrements taken from Yankee soldiers, living and dead. Like their lean, shaggy horses, they all looked in dire need of a washing and a good meal.

The officer, a captain, dismounted and approached the piazza, moving halfway up the front steps.

"We need food and horses," he said, after unceremoniously introducing himself.

"We scarcely have enough for ourselves," Mrs. Middleford answered him indignantly, offended by his blunt manner.

After she spoke, a few of the soldiers on horseback whispered among themselves, all the while frowning and staring at the ladies resentfully. Intimidated, Mrs. Middleford offered to provide them with some food "to take away" with them.

"Thank you, ma'am," said the gruff captain.

Within a few minutes, bags of corn, salt fish, and a few other edibles were brought out and given to the men. As soon as a share of the food was secured in their saddle bags, two young soldiers pulled away from the group and began trotting toward the stables.

"Where are those men going?" Mrs. Middleford demanded.

The captain shouted out an order for his men to return, and when it went unheeded, Harriott suddenly gave a cry of exasperation and followed after them, likewise ignoring her mother's frightened protests. She ran to the stable yard gates and barred them with her own body. The defiant soldiers, who reached the spot just seconds after she did, dismounted and faced her with determined expressions.

"Get out of the way, miss," said one, a homely, lanky young man with a dirty blonde beard.

"You will not have our horses," she declared angrily, heaving with panting breaths from her breakneck dash to the stables. "We've only a few, and they are old and feeble!"

"We'll see about that," the young man retorted.

"You will not!"

"Your army has need of them!" he bellowed.

"We have need of them!" she cried, glaring at him boldly, and showing no sign of relenting. "We have seen your orders from the government in the papers, that soldiers are not to impress the supplies that people have for their own use, unless ordered to do so by your commanding general. You have no such orders, and you disobey your captain!"

Harriott was fully as tall as the soldier, and they stood facing each other eye to eye. Under her unflinching, withering gaze, the man began to blink, and with each blink, looked less resolute. Finally, after muttering something about how he must yield to a woman, he nudged his companion, and both returned to their horses and rode back to join the others.

During the confrontation, the captain had assured the distraught mother that her daughter was in no peril.

"These are bad boys, ma'am. They frequently disregard commands, as you see, and do things that are wrong," he told her, "but they are the fiercest, bravest fighters I have ever seen, and I have never known them to harm a woman."

When his men were all together again, the officer shouted another order, and the company rode away. Harriott held a hand over her racing heart as she trudged back to the house. She was feeling a wave of weakness as her initial rush of passion and energy subsided, and was moving a little unsteadily. Her mother hurried down the steps to embrace her.

"That was very rash and foolish of you," Mrs. Middleford reproved her tearfully.

"But we still have our horses," said Harriott.

She heard the excited voices of her sisters, and they came rushing out of the house with little Gabriel in tow.

"Oh, Harrie!" cried Charlotte, "we saw and heard everything from the windows! Thank goodness those men are gone! We had to restrain Gabriel. He wanted to come down and protect you!"

Gabriel scurried over to his aunt Harriott and hugged her skirts.

"Thank you, dear," she said to him. "You are a good little man, but I do not think we were in much danger."

"How brave you were, Harrie!" Rebecca praised her. "We saw you stand that man down, and save our horses!"

"You were so very brave," Louisa agreed.

Mrs. Middleton, still shaken, did not agree, and repeated that it had been reckless of Harriott to confront the soldiers.

"Were you afraid, Harrie?" asked Rebecca.

"A little," she admitted, "but more for the loss of the horses than for myself."

"They were not like our Carolina gentlemen," Charlotte remarked somewhat indignantly. "Not a bit!"

"But still," said Rebecca, "their captain said they would never injure a woman, and there is certainly something fine in that."

* * *

A few days later, early in the morning, a neighbor arrived at the Briars bringing terrible news to the Middlefords. Several men had forced their way into the Clemonte house the night before and robbed the two sisters. Worse, these intruders had beaten both the women severely. A neighbor's manservant who was out hunting had heard their cries and entered the house after the robbers were gone, and the one sister who was still conscious told him that five soldiers had attacked them, one dressed in gray, the others in uniforms of blue. The man wearing the Confederate uniform had come to the door at supper time asking for food, claiming that he and his fellows were members of Captain Hyne's company. The ladies had heard of this unit out of Brevard, which was known to be hunting deserters, and agreed to provide a little food from their table. Unable to see the uniforms of the other men who waited in the darkness, the two sisters went to fetch them something to eat, and as soon as they did, all the soldiers rushed into the house.

Mrs. Middleford went very pale as she listened to this narrative. The Clemonte residence was nearby, and, like her daughters, she shuddered to think that these vicious men might have just as easily come to the Briars—or that they might return to the area at any time.

The Middleford girls set about making up a basket of food and other comforts for the unfortunate Clemonte sisters, the only topic of conversation among them as they worked being this horrible crime. Their mother disappeared to her room for a while, and later, just after the midday meal, she made an announcement to her family while they were still assembled at the table.

"I have written to your father," she said.

"Oh, Mama," Rebecca lamented. "I wish we could leave this place! Why must we seek his direction? By the time he makes up his mind—"

"I have not written to your father to ask his direction," her mother interrupted, in a nervous but firm, emphatic tone. "I have written to tell him that we are leaving Flat Rock. We shall travel to Columbia, and from there arrange lodgings in Greenville. It has become too dangerous in this place. I have made up my mind, and this is what we shall do, so I advise you all to begin packing the belongings you wish to take with you."

For a few moments, the girls looked to one another speechlessly, stunned by their mother's extraordinary decisiveness, then suddenly, all except Harriott abandoned their chairs and rushed off to make preparations for the journey.

"Mama!" Harriott cried admiringly. "I am so proud of you. I know you have made the right choice for us."

"Someone had to make a decision!" she sighed, looking troubled.

"Papa will understand," Harriott reassured her. "I shall write to him, and when I tell him of these latest outrages, I know he will approve of your decision, and will send us the money we will need."

"I have sufficient money for now," said Mrs. Middleton, surprising her daughter again. "I have been saving some for just such a contingency. Your father was able to send me some gold money from the sale of the rice crops, enough to last us for several months, but I shall use it, and all the other I have put aside, to take us back to South Carolina. In Columbia, I intend to sell some of my jewelry and some silver if I must. My family shall not go hungry, nor want for a safe place to live, I am determined."

"I'm glad Papa was able to send some money, but how I wish we could go home to see him, just for a little while," Harriott remarked.

"That we cannot do, nor will he leave to come and see us. Oh, I am so anxious for your father, and for all our people at home, but what can I do? Now go and make your preparations, dear, and write to Major Mitchell. He will be glad, I'm sure, to hear that we are leaving Flat Rock."

"He will be so glad, Mama! I shall go and write to him and to Papa this very minute."

* * *

In the spring of 1864, General Beauregard was ordered to Virginia, and he turned over his command in Charleston to another officer, General Jones. After a long inspection tour with the new general that required some travel by railroad, Major Mitchell returned to headquarters late one night in April. Seeing a light in the downstairs room that was used as an office, he looked in and saw Captain Wyatt still at work.

The young Englishman had been looking over some paperwork of the day, and, having just found several mistakes in a report that had been copied, was putting his hands to his head in a gesture of frustration.

"These clerks! These pups!" he grumbled, turning to the major with a nod of greeting. "Such carelessness! There should be a court martial for such clerical incompetence."

"And firing squads?" the major wondered facetiously.

"No, but perhaps some system of torture could be devised to

heighten accuracy."

James laughed, and the captain abandoned his vexation and joined him, his smile producing two deep dimples in his somewhat round, boyish face—a pleasant, very English face of fine complexion and coloring, crowned by golden brown hair that tended to cluster above the forehead in loose waves, and in curls around the ears.

"Why are you still working at this hour?" asked the major.

It was close to eleven o'clock.

"I had nothing else to do tonight," sighed the captain, and, suddenly feeling how late it was, he stood up and stretched his arms, displaying his tall, sturdy physique. His physical appearance, though one of great vigor and strength, was tempered by a gentle and diffident manner.

"Oh, by the way, Jim, a letter came for you today. I put it on your desk."

"From Flat Rock?" James asked eagerly.

"I think so."

The Englishman watched the major as he went to his desk, lit a candle there, and sat down to read the letter from Harriott. It was immediately obvious that it contained very good news.

"They're going to Greenville!" he exclaimed, looking up at the captain with an expression of relief and happiness. "They're on their way there now!"

"I'm glad to hear it."

"We can marry now, as soon as possible."

"Congratulations."

"You must come to the wedding, my friend."

"I doubt if I can get another furlough so soon," Captain Wyatt said regretfully. "I took one last month, you know."

"Well, I'm certainly getting one," the major laughed.

"I'm sure there's no doubt about that!"

James rested his cane against a chair and took off his hat and overcoat.

"Wyatt," he said, with a look of mysterious excitement, "I want you to see something."

"What's that?"

"I'm going to walk across this room without my cane."

"Let's see you do it, then, Major."

James walked the length of the room, turned, and walked back to his starting point, moving in a steady, normal manner.

"You didn't even limp," the Englishman commended him. "Well done, old man."

"I've been testing myself lately without the cane, and so far, so good, as you can see. There's some pain, but it seems to lessen each time I've put my full weight on the leg. It's much stronger now."

"I'm happy to hear it," said the captain, "but if I were you, I'd keep the cane for a while, at least until you're married. General Beauregard wanted you with him, and if he hears of your recovery, well, you might be joining him in Virginia—back into the fray and all that."

"I hadn't thought of that," James replied. "I've only been thinking how happy Harriott will be to see me well again. Nevertheless, back into the fray or not, I'm going to walk down the aisle of the church under my own power, and after the ceremony, I'm going to walk out with my bride on my arm, and without that damned stick!"

CHAPTER TEN

After a hurried exchange of letters between Charleston and Greenville, a wedding date was set.

Major Mitchell arrived in Greenville the day before the matrimonial event was to take place. Though tired out from a long journey by rail, he was suddenly invigorated and overjoyed as the train pulled into the depot, bringing Harriott and her family into view. They were waiting for him on the platform. A little unsure of his leg after many hours of sitting, he used his cane to step down off the car and walk to them.

After embraces and kisses from all the sisters, James was introduced to Harriott's uncle and aunt, Mr. and Mrs. Singleton, a kindly-looking couple in their sixties, and her cousin Miss Mary McCord, a pretty young woman of twenty-five who was wearing a carefully preserved hat of a style which had been the height of fashion just before the war.

Miss McCord took the major's hand and turned to Harriott with a waggish smile, remarking, "You have done well for yourself, cousin."

That evening, while a special supper was being prepared at the Singleton residence, Harriott took her fiancé outside to show him the little guest cottage which was to be their honeymoon abode. It was only a short distance from her uncle's house, but was somewhat secluded by trees and hedges. On the way, the major surprised and delighted her by hanging his cane over one arm and walking without it.

"How long have you been able to do that?" she asked him.

"For about a month now. I didn't write to you about it, because I wanted to surprise you."

"You did! And I'm so pleased!"

The guest house had a little garden, neglected and overgrown, but still pleasant, and they sat down there together on an ironwork bench to talk.

The major's expression grew very serious.

"Your sisters told me of what happened to the French ladies in Flat Rock, and your heroism when you saved the family's horses," he said. "I am surprised you did not write to me about these things."

His look made her wonder if he was displeased with her.

"I didn't wish to worry you," she explained, looking a little abashed. "And shortly after that happened, we made up our minds to leave Flat Rock."

The major gnawed at his mustache for a few seconds, ruminating, then remarked, "It pains me, Harriott, to think of you and your family in distress or danger, that is all. I wish I could be with you all the time to protect you, but I cannot, and that also pains me. Why doesn't your father—"

He stopped, his tone having grown testy, with brows contracted in frustration.

"My father is an old man," Harriott reminded him. "More than seventy years old. He believes he can do more for us, and for the country, by keeping our plantations productive."

The major breathed out a deep exhalation, and with it, seemed to expel his frustration. He put his arm around Harriott and kissed her hair.

"Forgive me, dear," he said. "I shall try not to worry about you so much now that you are here in Greenville."

"I feel so much safer here, and I've so enjoyed being with my cousin Mary. We are the best of friends, you know."

"She is a charming young lady," James remarked. "How old is she?"

"About five and twenty. Why do you ask?"

"I was wondering why she is not married or engaged."

"Mary is very particular about men."

"Too particular?" he asked.

"She doesn't think so," said Harriott. "Mary came very close to being engaged once, when she was much younger, but something hindered it. Apparently, he was an extraordinary young man, and I don't think she has ever found another as fine in her eyes, but she doesn't like to speak of it."

"I imagine I might know what happened," James ventured, looking thoughtful.

"Really? What do you think?"

"The young man's father disapproved. Was he also very young?"

"Why, yes. How did you know?"

"That's usually the way of it," he sighed. "It happened to me once. I believe my sister told you about it."

"She did. Sarah said she thought it may have been for the best, though. Do you think she is right?"

"Oh, probably, but at the time it was quite painful, and I was resentful for a long while afterwards."

James looked pensive and serious for a few moments, but

then shook himself, as if to shake off bad memories, and turned to Harriott with an affectionate smile and a kiss. They luxuriated in the happiness of each other's presence and closeness, and talked of the wedding that was to take place the next afternoon.

"As we are to be married tomorrow, I suppose you may call me Harrie now," she suggested.

The major drew back from her with a strange expression of revulsion and alarm.

"Oh, no!" he said emphatically. "I could never call you that. I have not told you so before, but I cannot bring myself to call you that. It is all right, I suppose, for your family and friends to do so, but I never could. The word will not form on my lips."

"Why not?" she asked, surprised.

"I cannot call you by a man's name. I shall call you Harriott, and my darling, and a thousand other endearments," he told her firmly, "but I will never call you—"

He caught himself, and they both laughed. She studied him, shaking her head with amusement.

"But there are any number of names that men and women share," she argued. "The name Francis, for instance."

"Yes, but it is spelled differently for ladies," he replied, in all seriousness, but aware that he sounded absurd. "Besides, you don't call ladies Frank."

"That's true," Harriott laughed.

Still holding each other, they gazed up at a blue sky, watching a few a noisy blackbirds flying over. Both of them thought of Flat Rock at the same moment.

"I imagine it is very lovely in Flat Rock now, with all the trees showing their new green, and the spring flowers beginning to bloom," she remarked wistfully. "I wish we could have had the wedding at the chapel there."

"Yes, I should have preferred that, too, but it is much safer here."

Despite its dangers, James also contemplated Flat Rock with affection and longing; it had only happy associations for him now. He said he wished he had some memento of the place now, and wondered if Harriott still had the little picture she had painted of the Briars.

"I put it in a frame and brought it here," she said. "And you may have it if you wish."

"I should like that. It will remind me of a most charming summer."

"It really isn't a very good painting, is it?" she asked.

He looked surprised, and seemed to search for an answer, finally replying, "It is a charming scene."

Harriott studied him with an amused, knowing look.

"When you said that you saw no common talent in my painting," she said, "it was a kind way of saying that my talent is just a little above mediocre."

James laughed, and the telling look in his eyes gave her his answer.

"You see, I have no illusions about myself as an artist. I see beauty, and want to reproduce it, but never can, to my satisfaction."

"Well, most art is aspirational, don't you think?"

"But some come closer to the mark."

"True," he said, "but I'm sure your writing is superior, and I should very much like to read your work someday if you will permit me."

"Why would think it is superior?" she asked.

"Because you are superior, Harriott."

For this she kissed him, and he kept an arm around her, holding her even closer as they enjoyed the beauty of the evening.

"Ah," he sighed. "How I wish this war was over, and you and I could live in Flat Rock in peace. I would buy a piece of land, one with a superb mountain view, and we would build ourselves a house that just suits our fancy."

"Oh, how wonderful!" she said, her imagination instantly captured by the idea.

"What sort of house suits you, my dear?" he asked.

Harriott mulled it over and came up with the notion of a home built in the style of an English cottage.

"I like that," he approved. "I see that our tastes are quite similar. Now, shall it be wood or stone?"

"Stone, I think."

"I prefer that, too. And what sort of roof?"

"Well...I suppose a thatched roof would be out of the question," she speculated whimsically.

"That would be very English, but certainly not practical. There is probably no one here who could make such a roof. Still, it's delightful to think of."

The two collaborated for nearly an hour constructing a future home, a place filled with all kinds of pleasant things—cozy rooms and fireplaces inside, and outside, a pond frequented by ducks and geese, or a stream of clear spring water and smooth stones running through the property, a long, wide piazza from which they could view the sunsets and clouds moving over the faraway mountains, vegetable and flower gardens, an orchard of fruit trees, a chicken yard...

"And a cat," said James. "You told me once that you are fond of cats, didn't you?"

"Yes." And Harriott added a handsome little feline to the sweet homestead now vividly pictured in her mind.

"We shall have that house someday," he promised her. "No

matter what, I am determined we shall have it. You may depend upon it."

Domestic dreams gave way to another pleasant subject, as they talked of the wedding that would take place the following day.

"The thought of it puts me into such a frenzy of happiness I doubt I shall sleep tonight," he told her, smiling affectionately.

"But you must be tired from your long journey this morning. You must rest," she urged him.

"I don't think my mind will rest, but I'll do my best to sleep. We can't have a haggard groom now, can we?"

"Certainly not. I won't stand for it. You will sleep tonight."

James laughed and kissed Harriott, then gave a salute.

"Well then, my bride has given me my orders, and I shall obey them."

* * *

When Major Mitchell returned to his duties in Charleston in late May, he found it very difficult to go back after a two week honeymoon with Harriott. It was such a change, such a contrast, to be torn from his bride's arms, and the peacefulness and spring beauty and greenery of the upstate, to return to his drab duties in a besieged city, much of which was in ruins from a great fire in the first year of the war, and from the effects of a relentless bombardment by the enemy. In 1863, the Federal forces had captured a position in the harbor, and from there had been throwing shells into Charleston nearly every day since mid-November of that year.

One June evening at dusk, Captain Wyatt walked into headquarters looking depressed and troubled. He was holding a letter he had just received and read.

"What is it, Wyatt?" the major inquired. "Bad news?"

The captain informed him that a letter from England

contained very bad news. There had been a death in his family. A favorite nephew had suddenly and unexpectedly passed away the previous month, the news having been delayed for a long time before it finally reached Charleston.

"He's been gone for weeks," said the Englishman. "And I didn't even know it."

"I'm very sorry," the major responded feelingly. "You have told me how much the boy meant to you. Is there anything I can do for you?"

"No, no," the captain whispered. "Thank you."

He went to his desk and began a letter to his sister in London, but after a few minutes, Major Mitchell noticed that he had stopped writing, and was simply staring down at the paper as if in a stupor. Another young staff officer brought in a report for him and, placing the papers on his desk, casually asked, "How's your history coming along?"

"My what? Oh, the history," said the captain, looking a shade less abstracted. "It's…coming along nicely."

The young man did not linger, but his question had reminded the other young officer of his duties, and he finished his letter to his sister and then turned his attention to stacks of papers before him, searching for some copies of correspondence that General Beauregard had written for.

Over the next few days, the Englishman was quiet and aloof during the hours in the office, and afterwards, in company, even more quiet, and no longer his usual cheerful, witty self. During this time Major Mitchell found it nearly impossible to begin a conversation with him on any subject other than department business, until one dull evening at their quarters, when, on a whim, he asked the captain to sit for a portrait.

"A portrait of me!" Captain Wyatt responded, surprised.

"You said you weren't much good at human figures. I am not a landscape or a building."

"I said that human figures didn't interest me as much," James corrected him. "I think however I could produce a good likeness of you. Let me try, won't you? It will help me keep my hand in, at least. I have an urge to paint, so oblige me."

"Whose property will the likeness be?" the captain inquired.

"Mine."

"Only if I approve of it," the captain put as a condition.

"Very well."

"Then I agree to it."

As the major readied his small supply of paints and brushes on his desk, he advised the captain to decide upon the pose he wished to strike.

"Where shall I sit?"

The artist positioned a chair between two lamps and seated his subject in it. "'Daylight would be much better, of course," he said, taking a seat at his desk. "But daylight is for other things."

"You haven't much paper," observed the Englishman.

"I have one small sheet of very good paper," James informed him. "Therefore I think your portrait must be something of a miniature."

"That shouldn't take long."

"We'll see," said the artist. "I must sketch you in pencil first. Now be still, and assume a comfortable but dignified posture."

"You will of course flatter me," the captain suggested, with the first semblance of good humor that James had seen in him in days.

"I will not," he answered decisively, amused. "You are no Adonis, but you do have an interesting face."

That night, and the next, Major Mitchell spent several hours on his little portrait, and when he was finished, showed it to his subject, who said it was a beautiful painting of an ugly fellow.

"Nonsense!" laughed the artist. "You are too hard on yourself. And to show you how wrong you are, I'm going to send this portrait to my wife, and get her opinion on it."

"Don't!" the other protested. "I don't approve of it, therefore it is mine, not yours."

"I'll give it to you after my wife takes a look at it," the major promised. "She hasn't seen any of my work, you know, and she'll be so pleased."

Despite the captain's continued objections, Major Mitchell sent off the picture to Greenville with his next letter. The following week, Harriott wrote back to him, reporting that she had showed Mary his little watercolor portrait of Captain Wyatt.

"I asked her what she thought of our English officer," she wrote. "She surveyed the picture very carefully and asked if it was a true likeness. I must confess, the question piqued me a little, but I trust I did not betray it. I told her that you do not flatter, if that what she meant. Well, if that is true, she said, her eyes still fixed upon the portrait, I think it is a pleasant face. I told her I thought it an honest face. That too, she agreed."

"How interesting," he thought. "Harriott's cousin likes his face."

Major Mitchell told the captain that his wife liked his face and the portrait, but did not tell him she had shown it to another lady, whose reaction to it had hatched an idea in his mind.

That evening, as James sat down at a desk to write a reply to Harriott, he took out a little leather case that held his only photograph of his wife. He had asked her to have her picture taken while she was in Columbia, and was very pleased when she presented it to him on their wedding day. He opened the case and sat the photograph in front of him on the desk as he wrote, pausing now and then to look up at her image.

Captain Wyatt, who was lazing in his bed, saw the major gazing wistfully at his wife's photograph and asked him if he had made up his mind to ask for another furlough.

"I think I have," said James. "It will do me good, and my absence of a week or so won't do much harm here."

The Englishman wondered if the weather was more pleasant in Greenville.

"It's somewhat cooler, I think," said the major.

He put down his pen and turned a thoughtful gaze on his companion, deciding that the time was ripe to carry out his little plan for the captain and Miss McCord, and suggested, "Say, Wyatt, why don't you come with me to Greenville?"

"A newly married man does not need my company," the captain chuckled.

"Well...I was only trying to be generous," James said mysteriously.

"What do you mean?"

"I mean that there is a certain young lady in Greenville who would certainly interest you."

The captain was immediately interested, but raised his eyebrows as if merely amused, and tried to sound nonchalant when he asked who she was.

"My wife's cousin, Miss Mary McCord," said James. "A very pretty, most charming lady—and a very sensible, intelligent young person like yourself. You two are about the same age, I imagine, and I think you would find her most congenial. I have told her about you."

"Really!" the Englishman chafed, pretending to be displeased. "What have you told her?"

"What else? I told her what an excellent officer you are, and that you are an interesting conversationalist, and altogether a fine, honest fellow," said the major, with a wry smile.

"Hm—m," the captain responded, looking a little wary.

"What harm could there be in meeting her? Didn't you say that the department had some business in Columbia, and that you would go there sooner or later? You could come up from there to Greenville on the cars. The countryside in that district is lovely, and perhaps you and I could do some shooting."

"Lots of game about there?" the captain inquired with evident interest.

"So I'm told."

"I wouldn't mind that," he admitted.

"Well then, there you are. I'm thinking of going up in August, if a furlough can be had."

* * *

A furlough was granted to Major Mitchell in the middle of August, and he had not been in Greenville more than a few hours when a letter came from Captain Wyatt, who was in Columbia, with news of his imminent arrival on tomorrow's train. The following afternoon, James and Harriott met him at the depot, along with Miss McCord. The major picked the Englishman out of the crowd that had just come off the cars, hailed him, and, after the two men exchanged a hearty handshake, the captain was promptly introduced to the two ladies, blushing like a girl when he spoke to Harriott's cousin for the first time. It was immediately obvious that he found her very attractive.

Miss McCord's plump face with small features gave an impression of primness, but she was very pretty, with a beautiful complexion, and large, dark blue eyes that sparkled with vivacity. She was a woman who had always attached much importance to good grooming and good clothes, and because of the scarcity of the latter, necessitating the wearing of old patched dresses and homespun, she lavished extraordinary care on her coiffure, and was given to frequent experiments and innovations in hair styles. Today, her dark auburn hair was pulled tightly to the back of the head and there gathered in a complicated coil, and her forehead was fringed with a series of identical ringlets lightly pomaded to keep their shape and place.

They took a carriage to the house that Harriott's family was renting, and that night Mrs. Middleford hosted a supper. Her younger daughters, delighted with the novelty of an English Confederate officer, continually peppered him with questions about England and its aristocracy and gentry, especially after they learned that Captain Wyatt's father was a baronet. Though somewhat embarrassed to be the center of attention, the young captain soon overcame his shyness and tried to answer all the inquiries put to him in an entertaining way. He conversed with Mr. and Mrs. Singleton, the major and his wife, and all the Middleford ladies lightheartedly and humorously; it was only when Miss McCord addressed him that his expression grew more serious and intent.

Mr. Singleton wanted to know about his life in the British Army and his travels abroad, so Captain Wyatt obliged him with interesting anecdotes, talking of comical incidents of camp life, the exotic scenes and customs of India and China, and travel adventures, including an encounter with bandits near Canton. Turquand and Gabriel were particularly fascinated by his stories. He did not speak of fighting or battles, and when Mr. Singleton asked him about a particular famous battle in India, the captain was suddenly tightlipped and unsmiling.

"I beg your pardon," he said, with downcast eyes, "but I should prefer not to speak of it."

"Certainly, Captain," Mr. Singleton responded apologetically. "Quite all right."

James broke an awkward silence that followed by changing the subject completely and asking Mr. Singleton about the legal aspects of a certain controversy going in the Confederate government. Full of concerns and speculations, the old gentleman was ready and willing to share them in conversation.

Later that evening, when they were alone in their cottage, Harriott asked her husband about the captain's unusual reaction to Mr. Singleton's inquiry about the Indian battle.

"There are certain things Wyatt has witnessed that he would prefer to forget, I suppose," he said. "I have read of some of the fighting and massacres he saw, and they must have been horrific. He really is a most tender-hearted fellow. He is a good soldier, yet he really hasn't the character of one, and I think perhaps his family expected it of him. He's spoken to me of some relatives and ancestors who distinguished themselves militarily."

"What profession would you choose for him?" Harriott wondered.

James mused a while, then answered, "A scholar I think. Yes, a scholar of some sort, or even a scientist. He's very intelligent and inquisitive."

While unbuttoning his coat, the major looked out a window toward the Singleton house, where, through the limbs and leaves of trees, he could make out the lights in the windows and occasionally, a figure passing by.

"I wonder if Captain Wyatt is finding his guest room comfortable," he said, chuckling a little.

"Why shouldn't he?" Harriott asked. "And what is so amusing?"

"I think he might find it a little uncomfortable to be under the same roof with your cousin Mary."

"Why is that?"

"Didn't you see how he looked at her? He's obviously much taken with her."

He turned to Harriott, and she slipped her arms around his neck.

"Is my husband a matchmaker?" she asked.

"Do you object?"

"No, I like the captain, but I wish you would include me in your schemes."

"Can you be trusted?"

Harriott laughed and kissed him.

"Ah, never mind," he sighed, pulling her closer. "Let's not talk of other lovers now."

* * *

Captain Wyatt passed much of the next day in the company of the Middlefords again at their house, along with James, Harriott, and Miss McCord, but in the late afternoon, thanks to some machinations by the major, he and Miss McCord were returned to her residence, and Mr. Singleton welcomed them into the parlor for some conversation before supper. The three had not even taken their seats before someone knocked at the door. The caller was a neighbor and a fellow lawyer who was seeking some advice about a difficult case, and he asked to speak to Mr. Singleton in private.

"My dear, will you entertain Captain Wyatt for me until I return?" he asked, tugging Mary toward the young man as he walked away.

"Certainly," she replied, letting her hand slip out her uncle's grasp before he could budge her very far.

She glanced toward a nearby sofa and invited Captain Wyatt to be seated. He waited until she took her place there, then sat down at a proximate but polite distance.

"Well, Captain," she began, "You said you are a recent addition to our army. Tell me, how long have you been in America?"

"I have been in the Confederacy about eight months now. I came into Charleston on a blockade runner out of Nassau."

"Oh! Was that exciting?"

"It was quite harrowing, Miss McCord. I don't recommend it."

She laughed, and he lifted his lips in a broad smile that produced a pronounced dimple in both cheeks, which were colored again with the same rosy blush she had seen on their first meeting, and several times since.

"Major Mitchell tells me that you met General Jackson in Virginia," she remarked.

"Yes, I had that honor," said the captain, growing more serious. "Just after I arrived in your country, I had to go to Richmond to seek a commission, and had with me a parcel of goods I brought from Nassau for the general—gifts from English admirers. He was gracious enough to receive me at his camp, where I spent one night in rather bad weather."

"What was your impression of him?" she asked very earnestly.

"He was all that you have heard, Miss McCord, and so gracious and kind to me, a stranger…"

As the young Englishman continued to talk admiringly of the famous "Stonewall" Jackson, Mary's eyes began to well with tears. When she pulled out a handkerchief and looked away, he paused.

"Forgive me, Captain," she said. "I was just thinking… as you spoke of your meeting with the general, that it was only a few months before he died."

Captain Wyatt swallowed hard and answered, "That is true. I see that you are deeply grieved by that loss, Miss McCord. I too grieved for him more than I can say."

Mary took a deep breath, dried her eyes, and tried to look composed.

The young man went on, "I have a letter General Jackson wrote to me which I value very highly. I wish I could show it to you, but I sent it home to England for safekeeping, along with a letter from General Beauregard."

"Whom you also greatly admire, I am told," she said, with the beginnings of a smile.

"Indeed I do," he declared proudly. "A first rate military man he is, and the perfect gentleman. I consider myself fortunate to have served on his staff. When President Davis gave me my commission, he offered me my choice of posts, and I chose Charleston, mainly because Beauregard was there."

"My uncle thinks the world of him, too. I only met the general once or twice, and found him very pleasant indeed. The last time I saw him was just a day or two before I left Charleston."

She took on a pensive look, and the captain guessed the cause of it.

"You miss Charleston very much," he suggested.

"I do," she sighed. "Almost my whole life was there, except for a few years when I was a child, which I do not even remember. I was born here in Greenville, but both my parents passed away when I was very young. I was raised by another aunt and uncle in Charleston, and when they died two years ago, I came back here to live with my uncle and aunt Singleton."

"I so admire your city by the sea," he said. "Even in ruins, it is beautiful."

After studying the captain for a few moments, Mary asked him curiously, "Why do you serve in our army?"

"To defend your country," he replied, simply and matter-of-factly.

"But you are an Englishman," she said.

"True, but I do admire your notions—and your ladies, or as President Davis styled you, *our incomparable women*. Without you, this war would have been lost long ago."

Mary studied the captain again, then opined, "I think you are chivalrous, so you fight for those who are outnumbered and less powerful."

He smiled at the compliment, but shrugged a little, as if not owning up to it.

"And you are modest," she added.

Another compliment brought another smile from the captain, along with the blush that her attention or admiration often inspired.

CHAPTER ELEVEN

The following evening, Captain Wyatt dined at the Singleton residence in the company of Mr. and Mrs. Singleton and Miss McCord. James and Harriott were spending the evening with her family. During supper Mr. Singleton inquired more about Captain Wyatt's experiences in China and India, and the young officer readily complied with more lengthy, interesting answers, having, it seemed, a limitless supply of intriguing or amusing anecdotes to draw on. After the meal, as the table was being cleared, he apologized, conscious that he had done most of the talking for over an hour.

"Heavens, Captain!" Mrs. Singleton protested. "No need for that. Your stories were much more delicious than our meal."

"Most entertaining," her husband agreed. "It is refreshing to hear of something other than this terrible war."

All returned to the parlor, where Mr. Singleton asked his wife to play the piano for everyone's enjoyment. He took his usual easy chair, and Captain Wyatt placed himself on the sofa beside Miss McCord (as close as politeness would allow), though there were several other chairs he might have chosen. As he took his seat, their eyes met, and the question that hers asked was answered by his in a fleeting look, *Yes, I wish to be near you.*

Mrs. Singleton chose a slow, serene sonata and began to play. Within five minutes, her husband was nodding off, and after a few minutes more, fell sound asleep. His legs were propped up on an ottoman, and a slight convulsion of one of his feet drew smiles from the audience on the sofa. Glancing in their direction, Mrs. Singleton detected the source of their amusement and smilingly shook her head as she finished playing the last notes of the sonata. In the silence that followed, a quiet snoring could be heard.

"Poor dear," said Mrs. Singleton, leaving the piano bench. "Mr. Singleton told me he did not sleep well last night, so I suppose it is catching up with him now. I shall go and fetch a coverlet for him."

She glided out of the room, leaving Captain Wyatt and Mary in the company of the sleeper.

"Is this the usual evening here?" the Englishman asked facetiously.

"Actually, my uncle usually lasts through the music, then falls asleep during my readings," Mary replied, in the same spirit.

"Not because your readings are dull, I'm sure."

"I hope not, though I daresay he would *not* nod off during one of your exciting stories."

"Oh, no, that is entirely possible, Miss McCord," the captain laughed. "I do go on too long sometimes, I know it. When I reach my dotage, I fear I shall be a most tiresome old man—one of those old fellows one hides in the bushes to avoid."

Mary laughed and told him about an elderly neighbor who exactly fit that description. Mr. Singleton stirred a little, and they automatically lowered their voices.

"What is your usual reading in the evenings, I wonder?" asked the captain.

"When Mr. Singleton is present, he prefers that I read histories and sermons. In his absence, my aunt and I prefer poetry and novels. We find such reading more diverting, and we sorely need diversion, especially in the evening, to keep unpleasant thoughts at bay."

"And which poets do you read?"

She named off a list of mostly English poets, including Herbert, Wordsworth, and Vaughn.

"Ah, do you know one of my favorites, Vaughn's 'Retreat?'" he asked.

"Oh, yes," she answered eagerly. "I do so like that poem."

He recited a few lines, and she drew back and surveyed him with overt curiosity and remarked, "I know you must be a very well educated man, but it surprises me that a soldier has such interests and tastes."

"I have many interests," he said, and then allowed himself to gaze deeply into her eyes, until she looked away. He asked her about her taste in novels.

"We haven't a large selection," said Mary, "but lately we have been reading works by Hugo and Mr. Simms."

"Simms," echoed the captain. "I have not read his work, but I have heard of him. Is he not from South Carolina?"

"Indeed he is. I think you will like his novels, especially the adventurous ones."

The captain drew back a little and studied her with a thoughtful expression.

"You think I am an adventurer?" he asked.

"Yes, partly," she answered tentatively, adding, "I mean, in the best sense of the word."

"Well, you are right, Miss McCord," said the Englishman, "and I hope I am that sort."

"I am sure you are. Mr. Singleton has expressed a very high opinion of you, you know, and I know him to be a very accurate judge of character."

Captain Wyatt beamed with obvious pleasure at her compliment as Mrs.Singleton returned with a quilt for her slumbering husband.

* * *

One morning, Major Mitchell took Captain Wyatt out on the shooting expedition he had promised. Hunting rifles in arm, they walked about a mile across a field and into some woods that bordered the property Mrs. Middleford had rented at the edge of town. The Englishman was quieter than usual, and seemed preoccupied. The major guessed why.

"Well, Henry, do you find that I represented Miss McCord accurately?" he asked.

"Yes, you did," the captain replied. "She is very pretty and very congenial, just as you said."

"You say that rather cooly. And yet I have never seen you blush so much as you have in her presence."

"Have I been blushing a great deal?" the Englishman asked uneasily.

"Like a beet!"

The younger man took a deep breath and closed his eyes. When he opened them he said dejectedly, "I suppose I ought to confess, then, since there is no hiding it from you. I am a lost man."

"A lost man!" James laughed. "That didn't take long, but I'm glad to hear it. You will owe me eternal gratitude for bringing you two together."

"But what if Miss McCord does not return my affection?"

"Oh, she likes you. I can tell."

"To like is not to love."

"How impatient you are!" the major marveled. "She's only just made your acquaintance. Woo her, man! Woo her and win her. I will tell you this piece of information. I know our ladies. They are not going to reveal any deeper interest until *you* do, even if they have such an interest. It would be considered forwardness."

"Yes, many English ladies are like that. Tell me, how did you know that I would fall in love with this lady?"

"I didn't know! I hoped that you would find her appearance and her company pleasant, and that if you did, perhaps a friendship might result, and eventually, something more, but I did not expect you to fall head over heels in love with her so quickly. I had no idea you were such a romantic fellow."

Captain Wyatt eyed his companion to discern whether he was being made fun of, but, seeing no sign of that, he sighed wistfully and began enumerating all the virtues and fascinations of "the charming Miss McCord."

The hunters saw little game that morning, and what little they saw was shot at and missed, so that both of them returned to the house empty-handed. On the day before their furlough was up, the two men went out hunting again. They were more successful this time, bringing home some game birds that were a welcome addition to the Middleford family table that evening.

At supper, on the eve of the officers' departure, everyone was talkative except for Captain Wyatt, though Mr. Singleton did manage to draw a brief story or two out of him. The next morning, James and Harriott left their little cottage and walked over to the Singleton house to collect the captain. It was time for the two officers to get to the depot to catch their train bound for Charleston. Before all the goodbyes were said, however, James and Harriott, working in concert, managed to draw away Mr. and Mrs. Singleton for a few minutes, leaving the Englishman alone with Miss McCord.

Though nervous and tongue-tied, the captain was able to express his gratitude for the family's hospitality. He told her how much he had enjoyed his time in Greenville, and Mary frankly acknowledged how much she and her family had enjoyed his company.

"But now I must return to Charleston," he said regretfully.

"You must come and visit us again if you have the opportunity," she responded, hiding her disappointment.

He looked down at the floor, and a silence followed.

"I...I wonder if I might write to you," the captain finally ventured, conscious that he was blushing again.

"You may," she answered, in a carefully measured tone, not wishing to sound too eager.

He thanked her, and they parted.

* * *

The captain's first letter to Mary arrived within a week. It began with news of the latest events in Charleston, but towards the end, he reminisced fondly about his visit to Greenville, and reminded her of their conversations about literature.

"I remember all we discussed," he wrote, "and a poem you might like came to mind, called 'The Great Adventurer.' Do you know it? It was something from Vaughn's time I think, though I do not recall the poet's name. Tell me what you think of this fellow."

The captain's letter ended with conventional, formal pleasantries, but Mary took the hint. She immediately searched out her anthologies of verse, found the poem he had mentioned, and read it. The last lines read thus:

You may train the eagle
To stoop to your fist;
Or you may inveigle
The phoenix of the east;
The lioness, you may move her
To give o'er her prey;
But you'll never stop a lover:
He will find out his way.

"He loves me," she thought, smiling and closing her eyes, "and he wastes no time in telling me so."

But how to answer, she wondered—not even asking herself the question, do I love him? She already knew that she did. Mary sat down and wrote a letter of reply, conveying what little news there was of goings-on in Greenville and describing some interesting letters from friends and relatives, and after a polite closing, she added the postscript: "It so happens that I did not know 'The Great Adventurer,' but I found it in one of my books. I know it now, and find the fellow very acceptable."

The captain's reply, which arrived the following week, made an open profession of his feelings for her, and from that point forward, an exchange of love letters began between the two. In early October, he managed a short furlough (combined with department business in Columbia), and took the train to Greenville. There, the first time he was alone with Mr. Singleton, he asked permission to seek Miss McCord's hand in marriage. Mr. Singleton was overjoyed, and instantly granted his request.

That evening, Captain Wyatt and Mary took a walk in the beginning shadows of twilight. They walked where two other lovers had recently walked, and sat where they had sat, on the iron bench near the guest cottage. There was no one occupying that little dwelling now; in Major Mitchell's absence, Harriott lived with her family, or stayed at the Singleton house.

As the two sat close together, the captain enjoyed the thrill of putting his arm around Mary for the first time. Soon, he became more ambitious.

"Now we are engaged, I wonder if I might kiss you," he said.

"You may kiss me," she replied.

And so he did.

"Sweet," he murmured in her ear, pressing his face against hers. "Can you feel how my heart is beating?"

She put her hand to his neck.

"Yes, I feel it."

"It beats for you, Miss Mary, and nothing else now—only you."

"You say such lovely things to me."

"I say what is true. I have found what I was meant for—to love you and take care of you."

"A man is meant for more than that," she demurred.

"It's true! There is more, but now that I have found you, I cannot imagine doing without you. Tell me, when shall we marry? Very soon, I hope. Is that possible?"

She looked surprised and hesitant.

"You are unsure of me?" he asked, with a pained expression.

"Oh, no!" she answered, but stammered a little as she tried to explain herself. "It's just that I thought—I thought—"

"You wished for a longer engagement, and more courtship," he said.

That was what she had wished, and expected. His wooing was very pleasant and sweet to her, but now, as Mary looked into his eyes, she felt that it was wrong of her to make him wait.

"I shall marry you as soon as you wish, dearest," she said.

"My next furlough?"

"Your next furlough."

His big smile produced the two deep dimples that she loved, and she put her hands to his face and pinched them. In return he pressed a kiss to her prim little mouth, and they talked of when another furlough might be arranged, and details concerning the wedding ceremony.

"I'm going to get a ring for you," he promised. "You *shall* have a wedding ring. I have a few gold sovereigns, and I'm going to have one made into a ring for you. What do you think of that, Miss Mary?"

She thought it was a very good idea.

* * *

At their wedding ceremony, which took place in Greenville in late November, Captain Wyatt presented his bride with a beautiful golden band, a ring fashioned out of a gold coin by a Charleston jeweler. They honeymooned at the Singleton guest house, but the end of a two week furlough brought the captain back to Charleston.

An unusually cold winter set in the following month, and around Christmas time, all of South Carolina was dismayed to hear of the fall of Savannah. Having ended his destructive march through Georgia, General Sherman had taken as his last spoil of war this beautiful city on the coast, and it was feared that his next target was the neighboring state of South Carolina. In early 1865, the general was known to be amassing a huge army for just such an invasion. By the first of February, the main advance of a force of over 60,000 enemy troops was underway, and there were too few Confederate forces in the state to offer any real resistance.

In Charleston, an evacuation began in the middle of February. All the Confederate troops left the city and began a march in the direction of North Carolina. About a week before they left the city, Major Mitchell and Captain Wyatt sent off letters to their wives.

"The enemy is destroying the railroads," wrote the major, "and we hear of great destruction to towns and plantations in their line of march. If we evacuate Charleston, and I expect that we will, I fear it will be difficult if not impossible to communicate with you for a while. It may be weeks before I can get a letter to you, dearest, but do not worry about me. I am fine. I have a good horse, and I am in the best of health. May God protect you all."

After these last letters from Charleston arrived in Greenville, many anxious weeks went by for Harriott and Mary with little word of or from their husbands. During this time, everyone was made more fearful by the news brought into Greenville by numerous refugees. Much of the city of Columbia had been reduced to ashes by Sherman's army, and afterwards, the enemy had continued its work of destruction in other towns and places in the state, until finally crossing into North Carolina. There had been some skirmishing with Confederate troops in the upstate of South Carolina (troops out of Charleston, it was reported), but it was not until the large army of General Sherman got into North Carolina that any battles of a significant scale took place, and once again, it was reported that the troops from Charleston were part of the Confederate forces fighting in these engagements.

In early March, Harriott and Mary were relieved when two reassuring but brief letters arrived from their husbands in North Carolina. On the same day, Mrs. Middleford also received a letter which contained bad news about her son Arthur. He had been captured during the winter, and was now a prisoner of war in Delaware.

Towards the end of March, an elderly gentleman, a neighbor

named Harrison, was at the door of the Singleton house with some news from North Carolina. He asked to speak with Mary. She received him in the parlor and they sat down there in the company of Harriott and her aunt and uncle. The neighbor told them that a young private furloughed because of his wounds, had passed through Greenville the day before. This soldier, who was returning from North Carolina, reported that he had heard of an Englishman killed in battle at Bentonville.

Mary's face went pale.

"Was he an officer?" Harriott asked urgently.

"My cousin didn't say," the neighbor replied. "He only knew that the man was an Englishman. I presume..."

The old gentleman stopped, thinking better of what he was about to say—that he presumed there were few soldiers of that nationality with the forces in North Carolina. He eyed Mary with concern, seeing how she was drooping, and looked about to faint.

"I don't believe it," she moaned. "I don't believe it. I won't! One of his superior officers, or some friend or chaplain, would have written to me."

"Perhaps one of them did," Mr. Harrison suggested reluctantly, "but there is no regular mail now. Perhaps a letter may have been sent by someone traveling in this direction, but Greenville is very far from Bentonville, and who knows what might have happened on the way..."

"No, no!" she cried in stubborn, tearful defense, bringing herself up to a straight, defiant posture. "I will not believe that man is my husband, until I have some official word."

"I'm very sorry to have distressed you, Mrs. Wyatt," the old gentleman apologized sadly. "But I thought I should tell you what I learned. Now I regret it very much. I ought to have waited, as you say, for some official word. I am very sorry."

Mr. Harrison's head was bent low, and he shook it again and again in self-reproach as he rose, turned, and slowly walked away.

As Mr. Singleton accompanied the neighbor to the door, Harriott and Mrs. Singleton, who were seated on either side of Mary, embraced her.

"You are right, Mary," Harriott encouraged her. "You are right to doubt him. All through this war, we have heard so many reports that turned out only to be rumors, and so many that were not true."

"Mr. Singleton knows of several Englishmen who were serving in Charleston," said her aunt, adding, "I remember so many times when we heard of some friend or relation who was reported to have been killed in battle, but then we found out he was only wounded, or captured, or none of those things. Battlefield reports can be very unreliable."

Mr. Singleton soon walked back into the parlor with a somber expression.

"Poor Mr. Harrison," he said. "He went away weeping. He has lately been shaken by news of a grandson's death, and says he has not been thinking clearly ever since."

"He was looking very feeble," Mrs. Singleton remarked. "Poor old thing—but I wish he had not come here!"

* * *

A few more tortuous days went by, and then, in the second week of April, a letter arrived, brought by hand from North Carolina by another wounded, returning soldier who lived near Greenville.

Mary saw her husband's handwriting and seized the young man's sleeve.

"He is alive?" she gasped. "Is he unhurt?"

The soldier assured Mrs. Wyatt that the captain was alive

and well. Harriott, who was standing beside her cousin, asked the messenger about Major Mitchell. The young man looked disturbed, and hesitated.

"Please tell me what you know," Harriott begged him.

"He was wounded," said the soldier. "Quite seriously, I understand. That is all I know. Perhaps the letter will give you more information than I can."

Mr. and Mrs. Singleton invited the young man to share a meal with the family, but he was anxious to be on his way, to get to his own family, and said he could not stay, only waiting long enough for a parcel of food that Mrs. Singleton insisted that he take with him. The older couple left the room with the soldier, leaving the two young women alone to discover what news the letter had brought.

Mary opened it with trembling hands. As Harriott stood close by, she read quietly for a few moments, and then raised her head with an expression of mingled relief and distress.

"Henry says that your husband was wounded in battle at Bentonville. The major has lost a leg, but he is alive, and my husband is going to try to send him to Camden as soon as he can travel."

"Oh, God," gasped Harriott, sinking into a chair. "Oh God, watch over him."

Mary went down to her knees and took hold of Harriott's hands to comfort her.

"He is alive, Harrie! He is returning to us! And my husband..."

Harriott tried to show some happiness for her cousin, but could only say haltingly, "I am so glad for you, dear. So glad—your husband has been spared to you."

"And yours has been spared to you, Harrie," said Mary,

managing at least a hint of a smile.

Harriott also tried to smile, but instead, thinking of the suffering that her husband must have endured, and the great danger he was in with such a terrible wound, she began to weep. She remembered a cousin who had died after losing an arm in battle, his life taken by infection less than a week after the amputation.

"Oh, Mary," she sobbed, "I thought I was happy, or at least content, before I met James. But now, if I lose him, I think I shall never be happy again in this world. I think I shall die, too, for I would not wish to live without him."

Closing her eyes to hold back tears, Mary tried to sound confident when she offered encouragement to her cousin.

"James is a strong man, Harrie. He will recover, and you two will have the rest of your lives together, I know it."

Recovering some composure, Harriott murmured, "Thank you. I must pray for him. I shall not cease to pray for him until I see him again. I must go to him."

"I shall certainly go with you to Camden," Mary said firmly."My husband's letter advises me to do that."

A little while later, Harriott went to Mr. Singleton to tell him the news of her husband and to see if arrangements could be made for transportation to Camden as soon as possible. He went out and made some inquiries, returning an hour later to report that a gentleman he knew was planning to return to Winnsboro by the end of the week.

"He is willing to go out of his way to take you and Mary on to Camden," said Mr. Singleton.

"That is very much out of his way," Harriott observed, looking doubtful.

"Don't worry about that. I have offered to pay Mr. O'Neal for his trouble. His house in Winnsboro was burned, and he is very much in need of money."

Harriott knew that her uncle and aunt were also in need of money, or would be soon enough, and it pained her for Mr. Singleton to part with any for her sake, but she was desperate enough to accept the sacrifice, and he was immovable that she should.

"Mr. O'Neal has a wagon, and knows the roads well," Mr. Singleton went on. "He will have his son with him, a boy of fourteen, and they will protect you, but I must insist that you and Mary also carry arms to protect yourselves. My wife is much against this journey, you know, and fears for your safety."

"Yes, I know…she wishes us to wait—but for what?"

"Until the railroads are running again."

"Heaven knows how long that may be! I cannot wait so long. I must go to him."

"I understand, Harriott," Mr. Singleton said tenderly. "I would do the same. Do what you must."

That evening, Harriott's mother and sisters came over, bringing news about Arthur, who had written from Fort Delaware to report that he was in good health. Mrs. Middleford had also received a letter from her husband. His plantation had been burned by the enemy, and the old man had walked most of the way from Georgetown to Columbia, and would soon travel from there to Greenville by wagon with some relations.

After supper, the entire family gathered in the parlor to offer thanks to God and pray for all their absent loved ones.

CHAPTER TWELVE

The trek to Camden was long and difficult, at times dangerous, and sometimes miserable because of bad weather, and worse, along the way, terrible rumors came to the travelers' ears about a Southern surrender in Virginia, but they all refused to believe these reports, and journeyed on until Mr. O'Neal's wagon finally reached its destination one chilly, overcast morning. Camden was one of many towns in the state which had been visited by the destroyer, and Harriott and Mary sadly observed the ruins of a number of burnt buildings as they drove in.

Mr. O'Neal pulled up at a large handsome residence on Hobkirk Hill, where he and his son dropped off the passengers, unloaded a few pieces of their baggage, and then continued on to a relative's house in another part of town.

The two women walked up the steps to the front entrance and knocked. An old, stooping black man opened the door.

"Are you Stephen?" Harriott asked him.

He eyed the two women warily and nodded.

"I am Mrs. Mitchell," she said. "Is my husband here?"

"No'm," he muttered.

"You came up from Charleston?" she inquired.

He nodded again, and a voice from inside the house made him turn around. Stephen stepped out of the way, and Harriott found herself standing face to face with another Mrs. Mitchell, her mother-in-law.

"Come in," said the lady.

Harriott and Mary stepped inside and introduced themselves.

"Since I heard from my son," said the elder Mrs. Mitchell, "I have been expecting you, Harriott—and you, Mrs. Wyatt."

The elder Mrs. Mitchell was a tall, dignified woman dressed in black clothing. Harriott later learned that she was in mourning for a grandson, one of Mrs. Stiles' boys. Her hair was a mixture of salt and pepper, but her heavy eyebrows were still soot black, and her stern, plain face was somewhat forbidding, until she smiled.

She took Harriott's hand and kissed it, smiling at her tenderly.

"I am so glad to meet my new daughter," she said. "You are just as my Jimmie described you. I am very pleased."

Harriott was bold enough to reach out and put her arms around the old lady briefly.

"Is he expected soon?" she asked.

"We expect him any day now, any hour really," said Mrs. Mitchell. "When I saw your wagon from the window, I thought it might be him, but it is good that you are here now to greet him."

Harriott asked about Mrs. Stiles, and before she finished her question, that lady appeared on the stairs, also dressed in black, and slowly descended to greet her sister-in-law.

* * *

At supper that evening, Mrs. Stiles was quiet and subdued. Her mother explained to her guests that Mr. Stiles and his eldest son were prisoners of war in Maryland. She had told Harriott of the death of the younger son earlier in private.

"Let us hope they will be released soon, Sarah," Harriott offered comfortingly. "My brother Arthur is a prisoner at Fort Delaware, but thank God, he is alive, and I know he will return to us."

Mrs. Stiles murmured faint thanks, and gradually, little by little, she joined in on the evening's conversation, though she only drank a little water, and ate nothing. The meal was very simple, even meager, and there was no meat on the table.

As Harriott became better acquainted with her mother-in-law, she found that she was beginning to like her. Though the old lady was highly opinionated and somewhat temperamental, she could also be very kind and compassionate—except when it came to Yankees, a subject that Mrs. Stiles brought up towards the end of the meal when Harriott noticed the absence of her wedding ring.

"They raided our house, and insulted us horribly," she said. "They took my jewelry, all our valuables, really, except for the silver we were able to hide, and some of the servants went off with them."

"How terrible!" Mary commiserated.

The elder Mrs. Mitchell looked extremely grim and suddenly brought down a hand to the table with a loud slap.

"Sarah!" she cried angrily. "I told you we shall not speak of it! We shall not speak of it!"

After this, Mrs. Stiles grew quiet again, and when the meal was over, she excused herself and went upstairs. Mrs. Mitchell took Harriott to another part of the house to show her a room which had been prepared for the major. A bed had been brought into a study on the first floor, and a nightshirt, a robe, and a few other pieces of clothing and bandages were laid out on it.

"I imagine it will be difficult for James to go up and down the stairs for a while," she explained. "And we shall be able to take care of him better here."

Harriott noticed that there was also a daybed in the room. Then she noticed on the wall above this piece of furniture, a small painting, a landscape, and suddenly remembered the two pictures her husband said he had sent to Camden for safekeeping.

She pointed to the painting and asked if it was one of his works.

"Ah, yes," said Mrs. Mitchell, with evident pride. "It is one of several that we were able to hide from the raiders. We concealed two of his larger works behind a heavy old sideboard, and painted the sides of the frames to make them look like part of the furniture."

"Are they his paintings of the forts in Charleston?"

Mrs. Mitchell smiled in answer and took Harriott's arm to lead her into an adjoining room. There, on the wall opposite the door where she entered, hung two sizeable paintings encased in what had once been handsome gilt frames. Harriott drew closer for a better view, and stopped, lost in admiration.

"They are beautiful," she said feelingly. "And just as James described them to me. So beautiful!"

"Aren't they?" Mrs. Mitchell agreed, coming to her side. "My son has great talent, I think."

"There is no doubt about that!"

One of the paintings was a scene of human action in broad daylight, the other, a seascape at twilight. The first depicted a scene at Fort Moultrie; the second was a view of Fort Sumter, showing the imposing stronghold in Charleston harbor as it had looked before being battered and reduced to rubble. A fiery sunset sky streaked with the foreboding color of blood bathed the structure in a rosy golden light, while a small vessel passed before its guns in glassy waters.

The paintings were realistic, and yet there was an element of romance about them, if only in the drama they portrayed. The colors were striking and dramatic, and Harriott was especially impressed by the backgrounds of the heavens—the colorful, tempestuous dusk, and the luminous, cloudless blue sky of the Fort Moultrie scene, against which the massive walls and interior of the fort glowed in bright sunlight. Figures in grey uniforms went about their duties as their guns sent shells into Fort Sumter before its surrender.

"James wished to present one of the paintings to General Beauregard," Mrs. Mitchell remarked, "and the general said that he would be honored to accept it, but advised my son to send them out of Charleston until the war was over."

"I'm so glad you were able to save them," said Harriott. "Now that I have seen them, it would break my heart to lose them."

Harriott moved closer to the paintings, close enough to see the brush strokes, and was about to make another observation about them, when suddenly, a knock at the front door sent all the women flying to the entrance hall. Mrs. Mitchell opened the door, and there stood Harriott's cousin, Dr. Frost.

"I beg your pardon," he said, tipping his hat to the elder lady. "I heard that my cousin Miss Middleford, I mean, Mrs. Mitchell, was here, and I wished to see her."

Surprised to see her cousin in Camden, Harriott rushed out to embrace him, and brought him inside to make introductions. He explained that he had been furloughed because of illness, but had now recovered, and was planning to return to his brigade soon. Harriott told him that they were expecting her husband any time now. When the doctor learned that the major was seriously wounded, he offered his services as a physician.

"Unfortunately," he added, "I have a wide experience with such things."

Both of the Mrs. Mitchells expressed their gratitude and invited the young surgeon to stay a while. Dr. Frost, however, did not linger long. He said he was on his way to check on another patient, but before leaving he asked Harriott about her family (with Louisa particularly in mind, she discerned).

"They are well," she said. "Lou is very well, and sends you her love. All the family does. They hoped that I would see you here eventually, and find you well."

"I am," he replied, looking relieved and moved. "Send for me as soon as your husband arrives, Harrie, no matter what hour."

* * *

About nine o'clock the next morning, a rickety old wagon pulled by two equally rickety old mules slowly rambled up the carriage drive and came to a stop. The driver, Captain Wyatt, jumped down, opened the back of the wagon, and helped Major Mitchell get out. Mary, who was seated by a window, was the first to see them, crying out for Harriott and Mrs. Mitchell as she rushed to the door.

Mary ran to her husband, but abruptly stopped in her tracks when she saw that one of his arms was in a sling. He was supporting Major Mitchell with his other arm as the latter situated himself on a pair of crutches.

One leg of the major's threadbare trousers was pinned up at the knee. The leg which had been injured years ago in another battle—the one he had struggled so desperately to save, and worked so hard and so long to reclaim—was gone. The stubble of several days' growth of beard covered his cheeks and chin, and Captain Wyatt also looked badly in need of a shave.

"Oh, Henry! We have been so anxious for you both," Mary said tearfully. "James, you must come inside at once!"

The major nodded wearily, and the captain threw a ragged

blanket over his shoulders and guided him toward the front steps of the house. Harriott and Mrs. Mitchell were at the door by now, and came out to assist him, but Captain Wyatt gently interposed and steadied him as he mounted each of the four steps on his crutches. At the threshold James paused, hanging his head in exhaustion, but a kiss from Harriott drew a faint gurgle of pleasure from him, along with a kiss and a caress from the other Mrs. Mitchell.

He looked so pale and tired that his mother insisted that he immediately be put to bed. He asked for Stephen, his father's old manservant.

"I shall help you, dear," Harriott said anxiously. "Let me help you."

"No, no, I wish Stephen to help me—only Stephen," he insisted.

The old black man was just coming into the room as his name was repeated. He had been told of the terrible wound, and, seeing the major's condition, he compressed his lips and contracted his brows in an effort of self-control, but was unable to speak.

"Stephen," James greeted him. "It is good to see you again. Please assist me now in undressing. I must rest."

"We have a room prepared for you on this floor, dear," Harriott told him.

"Thank you," he sighed. "I shall send for you ladies presently."

They watched him follow Stephen into the study, until its door closed behind them.

"He doesn't wish us to see his—his injury," said Mrs. Mitchell.

Harriott turned to Captain Wyatt and asked him about her husband's condition.

"He has been doing well as can be expected after the

removal of his limb," the Englishman replied. "The journey here was hard on him, but I think he only needs rest and time. He will do much better now that he is home, and in your care."

Mary was still holding on to her husband, and would not let go of him. He led her into the adjacent parlor and sat down with her on the sofa, where they remained in an embrace for a while without speaking. After a few minutes, Harriott went in to the room to find out more from him about what had happened to her husband. She pulled up a chair facing the couple and asked Captain Wyatt some questions.

He told her that Major Mitchell had been shot through the leg in the early part of the fighting at Bentonville. His horse had also been shot, and fell with him, causing even greater injury to the wounded limb.

"They had to remove his leg," he said. "Or else he would not have lived. I saw him fall, and went to him immediately, and saw to it that he was carried off the battlefield to a field hospital. There were many, many wounded, but I made sure the surgeons gave him prompt attention, and after the fight I stayed with him as much as I could."

Harriott grasped his hands and expressed her gratitude in a choking, tearful voice. Mary, who still clung to her husband, reached out and gently stroked her cousin's hair.

"He was in such terrible pain," the captain continued quietly. "He thought he was dying, and it was plain that you were uppermost in his mind, Harriott. He seized my hand and asked me to convey a message to you. He said, tell my wife, that I love her devotedly, and regret leaving her more than I can say. Almost before the last of these words left his mouth, he fainted away with the pain, and was taken away to be operated upon."

Picturing her husband's suffering, Harriott covered her face;

Mary also wept and buried her face in the captain's sleeve.

Affected by their emotion, he went on in a shaky voice, "When he woke up from the operation, he seemed surprised to find himself alive, and from that moment he was adamant that he would recover and return to you. Now that he is with you, he'll recover quickly, I'm sure. He's going to be fine, Harriott."

As she wiped her tear-drenched face with a handkerchief, the captain studied her, and his weeping wife, with a hesitant, pained look.

"What is it?" asked Harriott, seeing that something else was on his mind.

"You have heard the rumors?" he said after a pause.

His wife looked up with a horrified, disbelieving expression, and Harriott's hand went to her mouth, as if to suppress a cry.

"They are true," the captain whispered. "Lee has surrendered. I've no doubt that General Johnston will be forced to do the same with his army, if he has not already done so. It is over."

* * *

Stricken and grieving, Harriott went into a room next to the one her husband occupied and waited to see him. He had already been with Stephen a full half-hour, and after another half-hour passed, Harriott began to grow impatient. Mrs. Mitchell, who had been looking for her, came in with Mrs. Stiles and said that Stephen must be bathing James. The ladies sat down next to Harriott on a sofa, and they waited in silence.

Mrs. Mitchell had been told about the surrender, but said nothing on the subject, and seemed to bear it stoically. Harriott remembered, however, what Mrs. Stiles had told her about her mother's character, and suspected that the lady was suffering as deeply as everyone else in the household.

After a few more minutes, the old servant emerged from the

room holding a basin of water, with a damp towel draped over one arm. He told the ladies that the major was ready to receive them.

Harriott immediately moved toward the door, but Mrs. Mitchell and Mrs. Stiles kept their seat.

"Mother," said Harriott, glancing back at her, "aren't you coming in?"

"It's you he wants to see now, dear," Mrs. Mitchell replied. "He needs you. Go to him. We shall see him presently."

Needing no further encouragement, Harriott quickly went into her husband's room. James was sitting up in the bed, propped up by several pillows behind his back. Bathed and clean-shaven, except for his mustache, he smelled faintly of soap, and his hair was wet but neatly combed. He was smiling, but looked thin, fatigued, and weak.

She had never seen him look weak before.

"Come here," he said.

Harriott rushed to the side of the bed and sank into his arms. James trembled as he held her tightly to himself, and she felt him catching his breath in sobs.

"Harriott," he sighed. "All is well now, now I am with you."

"We'll take care of you," she said tearfully. "You shall be well."

She drew back from him a little to look into his eyes. He smiled again, blinking away tears.

"As you see, I have lost a limb."

"It doesn't matter, as long as you are well."

"The old lion tried to devour me," said James, "but he only got a leg, and I can do just as well without it. It had never completely healed from the first wounds, you know, so I didn't regard it as any great loss."

"Only a soldier would say such a thing," she replied with a

tender, trembling smile, putting her hands to his pale, drawn face.

He kissed those hands and held them in his own.

"What a beautiful sight you are, Harriott," he said. "The most beautiful sight in the world to me."

She kissed him, murmuring his name.

"Harriott, after I was wounded, I thought I would never see you again in this world, and that caused me more agony than the pain of my shattered leg. You know...the doctor told me I was delirious for a while, and called out your name again and again. When I realized that I might survive, I know it was the thought of you that helped me most."

"I prayed for you, night and day," she whispered, her voice strangled with emotion.

James asked Harriott about her family, and when she could speak again, she began to relate all the news. All the while, his eyes were fixed on her greedily, and never left her.

"I'm very glad to hear about Arthur," he said, after she told him about her brother's last letter. "I know it is great relief to all of you to know he is all right."

"Oh, we are so thankful!" she said. "If he had not been a prisoner of war, he might not have been spared to us, for we heard that his regiment suffered terrible losses in a battle that occurred just after his capture. Mama said it was providential."

"What about about Charlotte's young man?" asked James. "Any news of him?"

"Yes," Harriott answered with a saddened expression.

"Ah, bad news?"

"You know Mama did permit them to correspond, but after January, we heard nothing from Lieutenant Wilson for months. Then at last Charlotte received a letter from Columbia, from his father. He had found one of Charlotte's last letters to him, and wanted to let her know that his boy was at home convalescing from wounds."

"Was he hurt very badly?"

"He lost an arm, and suffered a wound to one of his eyes which has taken away some of his sight."

"Poor boy! How did Charlotte take the news?"

Harriott slowly shook her head, taking on a look of wonderment and pride.

"Lottie," she said, "was magnificent. Nothing seemed to shake her devotion. She told us that they had pledged themselves to each other, and considered themselves engaged. Lieutenant Wilson's father, however, wrote to her that under the circumstances, his son would understand if Charlotte wished to be released from their engagement, and wanted to know her wishes in the matter. She wrote him and replied that she loved his son and would not break off the engagement unless he no longer loved her."

"They are still engaged?"

"They are. I suppose the young man thought that a girl so young might not want a man in his condition, and so he felt obliged to release her. But he really didn't want to lose her, you see."

"Of course he didn't," said James, smiling feebly. "Lose a magnificent Middleford girl? That would be too much for any man to bear."

* * *

Dr. Frost was notified of Major Mitchell's arrival, and after quickly finishing up some other work, he came to the house in the early afternoon. Following the examination of his new patient, the young surgeon talked with Harriott and her mother-in-law.

"Wes, tell me—tell us the truth. Is he in any danger?" asked Harriott.

"In my opinion, no," he replied. "According to Captain

Wyatt, he was doing well in the hospital after the crisis passed, but the journey here exhausted him. He was cautioned that he was not ready to travel, but was so determined to get home, he did not heed these warnings. He is suffering for it now, but I think it is only a temporary setback. His leg is healing well, and there is no sign of infection."

"Oh, thank God," she sighed.

"He needs to rest a few days, but not too long. As soon as he feels up to it, he should take a little exercise, walk with the crutches, a little more each day, and spend less time in the bed and more time sitting up in a chair. This will help him regain his strength. He seems very willing and anxious to be well again, and I see no reason why he shouldn't."

Harriott thanked the doctor profusely, and the elder Mrs. Mitchell offered him something to eat. Dr. Frost seemed interested, but he hesitated.

"We are not complete paupers, Wes," Harriott assured him. "You must allow us to repay you at least a little today. We are so grateful to you!"

"Well...um," he mumbled, tugging at his goatee, but before he could say another word, the two ladies were leading him into the dining room.

There, Harriott ate only a few bites rather hurriedly, while the other Mrs. Mitchell went to spend some time with the convalescent. When her mother-in-law re-appeared in the dining room, Harriott promptly left and went to her husband.

"Dr. Frost gave me such good news about you!" she said happily, greeting James with a kiss to the forehead.

"Did he? What did he say?" he asked.

She sat down on the edge of the bed and repeated all that the physician had told her.

"That's exactly what he told me," the major observed. "Except that he called me a stubborn fool."

"You are stubborn, dear," she laughed, "but it made me so happy and hopeful, to know for certain that you will soon be well."

"Dr. Frost is going to see about a wooden leg for me. He knows a very skillful man here in Camden who will make me one. Then I shall be able to walk again without the crutches."

"That is also good news, but first you must regain your strength."

"Oh, yes, I know," he said, breathing out a weary exhalation, and slowly closing and reopening his eyes.

"You should rest now," she urged him, taking one of his hands and pressing it to her face.

"I am feeling sleepy," he sighed, "but I don't wish to be parted from you. You will stay with me, Harriott, won't you?"

"I will, darling."

With another long sigh, James reclined his head against the pillows and closed his eyes in a drowsiness that was quickly overtaking him. When his breathing took on the regularity and character of deep sleep, Harriott inched off his bed and made herself comfortable on the nearby daybed, where she also eventually closed her eyes in slumber, sleeping more soundly and peacefully than she had in months.

CHAPTER THIRTEEN

News of Major Mitchell's return spread about the town, and relatives and neighbors soon began stopping by to bring small parcels of food and other necessities for him and the family. Knowing that these kind people could ill afford to spare such things, his mother tried to refuse at least some of them, but she was always overruled.

One afternoon, their closest neighbor, an extremely elderly, retired clergyman, paid a visit. He came empty-handed, but told Mrs. Mitchell that she and her family were constantly in his prayers.

Mrs. Mitchell thanked the old gentleman, but she had received him rather cooly, and as they took their seats and conversed in the parlor, Harriott discerned that he was not the most welcome of guests in this home.

"How thankful I am," said the old man, in his wavering, weak voice, "that your son has returned to you. It is one thing to be thankful for, my good lady, although we are groaning under very severe afflictions now. We must, however, accept this awful defeat of our country as the will of God, and trust—"

"The will of God!" Mrs. Mitchell interrupted in a low, vehement voice.

"Well, my—my good lady," the neighbor stammered, looking disturbed.

She slowly rose from her chair to her full, impressive height, her dark eyes flashing with anger.

"Is it the will of God that men should murder and plunder their brethren—impoverish half the states? I think not! As you are a minister, Sir, you know who the god of this world is. It is *his* will that has been done in this war!"

And, turning away wrathfully, Mrs. Mitchell stormed out of the room, leaving Harriott and Mrs. Stiles to see the thoroughly abashed old gentleman to the door. As the clergyman was leaving, Dr. Frost was just arriving, holding a pair of crutches under one arm. He tipped his hat to the minister, perceiving his embarrassment (and that of the ladies), but Harriott bid goodbye to the one and invited the other in in as if nothing was amiss.

"I've brought some better crutches for Jim," he said. "I noticed that the ones he had were rather old and rough. These should be much more comfortable."

Harriott thanked her cousin and insisted that he accept some payment for them.

"No, no, Harrie," he objected. "They didn't cost me anything. A convalescent soldier who no longer needed them gave them to me. He told me to pass them on to someone who did need them."

"How kind of him," said Mrs. Stiles. "You must convey our thanks to this soldier."

"I'll do that, but first let me have a look at your convalescent."

Harriott accompanied Dr. Frost to her husband's room, but before going in to his patient, the doctor paused at the door.

"Will you wait for me, Harrie? I'm just going to check his bandages, and see if he is in any pain. It won't take very long. I want to speak with you privately about something—else."

"Certainly, Wes," she replied. "I'll wait for you next door."

Harriott went into the adjacent room and sat down on a sofa that faced the two paintings of the Charleston forts. Within ten minutes, her cousin walked in, and though he looked preoccupied at first, his attention was immediately drawn to the works of art that met his eyes.

"Are these your husband's paintings?" asked Dr. Frost.

"They are."

"Beautiful," he said admiringly. "I had no idea...how very beautiful."

"I think so, too," said Harriott.

He made a closer inspection of the paintings, murmuring more praises, but soon took a seat beside Harriott and, growing serious, changed the subject.

"Harrie," he said, in a confidential, somewhat urgent tone. "May I speak with you about a personal matter?"

"Of course, Wes. What is it?"

"I—I asked Lou to marry me again," he said, turning his eyes to the floor. "I wrote to her last month, and asked her. Last week, I received a reply from Greenville. She only said that she would like to see me again. But Harrie, it's impossible for me to get to Greenville now. I couldn't possibly go until the railroads are in operation again. My father is very ill, and there are many others here under my care now."

"I'm sure she knows that."

"Believe me, I shall go as soon as humanly possible, but...I want to know your opinion. Do you think I have any hope?"

"I think her answer very hopeful for you, Wes," Harriott reassured him. "First of all, she did not refuse you. She did not decline your proposal."

"That's true!" he said, suddenly looking up with a trembling smile.

"The fact that she did not refuse you, tells me that she is considering your proposal. And the fact that she wishes to see you, tells me that she wishes to determine, by seeing you and speaking with you face to face, whether her feelings for you might have changed, or could change, in your favor."

"You know her better than anyone!"

"I think I do, and I think she will be favorable toward you."

"Oh, Harrie!" he said, putting his arms around her. "You don't know how happy this makes me!"

"But I do, Wes!" she laughed. "And I am so happy for you."

* * *

Once Captain Wyatt's wounded arm was sufficiently healed, he and Mary decided that they would return to Greenville. Visiting the major's room one afternoon, they told the Mitchells of their plans.

"What will you do there?" asked James, wondering how the young man was going to support himself and a wife.

"I don't know," the captain replied with a shrug. "It has been Mary's home for a long while now, and she has belongings there, and family of course, but I don't know that we will stay. Ultimately, I don't know what we'll do."

"We shall miss you both," said Harriott. "And I shall always be grateful to you, Henry, for helping my husband and bringing him home to me."

The modest Englishman blushed and smiled a little, and his wife patted his dimpled face affectionately, then took her cousin's hand.

"Oh, Harrie," sighed Mary. "I hate to part with you. Perhaps you and James ought to think of coming back to Greenville, too.

Your mother and sisters wish it, I'm sure."

"I am not certain they will be there much longer," said Harriott. "But who knows? Perhaps we shall go back."

Three days later, there was a tearful parting of the two cousins. One began a journey to the upstate with her husband, while the other remained in Camden with hers.

Over the next few weeks, the major followed his doctor's orders and began spending a little more time each day out of bed. Soon he was passing much of his time not only sitting up in an easy chair, but also walking around the house, and outdoors, on his crutches. James was looking stronger, and putting on weight, yet as his physical health improved, he gradually became more depressed in mind and spirit. He found any news of the dire conditions in Charleston and the rest of the state (now under military occupation) unbearable. He was almost glad for his confinement as a convalescent, as it insulated him somewhat from the outside world, at least temporarily.

He wanted Harriott with him as much as possible; she seemed to be his only comfort, but eventually he grew somber even in her company, and she found it more and more difficult to think of anything to cheer him. There was little in their world now to inspire cheerfulness.

CHAPTER FOURTEEN

A letter from Mrs. Middleford brought news that she and the rest of the family had moved back to Columbia, and would live there for a while with a relative. Dr. Frost's father had recovered from his illness, and another army surgeon had just returned to Camden to resume his old practice, so Weston decided to make a trip to Columbia to see Louisa.

"I must go now," he told Harriott one day. "I must know, once and for all, if Lou will have me. How can I go on loving her to no avail? The thing must be settled once and for all."

Dr. Frost traveled in the company of another man who was bound for Columbia, and arrived there early one Saturday afternoon. The young doctor observed the condition of the city with shock and dismay. A large portion of the place had been burned by Sherman's army in February 1865, and though a little rebuilding had begun, the desolation he saw was still appalling.

The Middlefords were residing with Mr. Middleford's brother, whose house had been pillaged but spared the torch. Dr. Frost parted ways with his traveling companion a few blocks away from this address and walked the rest of the way.

As he turned a corner and approached the house, Mrs.

Middleford happened to be standing in the piazza talking with a lady he did not know. When she recognized Weston, her hands immediately went to her face, and her eyes welled up with tears of happiness. He rushed through the open gate, put down his medical bag and a valise, and was instantly in her arms.

"Weston, Weston," she sobbed. "How good it is to see you again, my boy. We have all been longing to see you."

"I am so glad to be with you again," he said.

As Mrs. Middleford released him from her embrace, Dr. Frost was introduced to the lady, an elderly neighbor. She had been on her way out as he arrived, and did not linger.

"Where are the girls?" he asked Mrs. Middleford. "Is everyone at home?"

"Mr. Middleford is away, and Charlotte and Rebecca, but Louisa is home with me at present."

They walked into the house, and Mrs. Middleford explained that her husband and his brother had gone to Winnsboro to visit a dying sister.

"Rebecca and Charlotte," she went on, "are visiting at Mr. Wilson's house."

"How is he?" asked Dr. Frost.

"The young man is recovering, slowly, I am told. Charlotte goes to see him nearly every day. Her father was escorting her before he had to leave, and now Rebecca or Louisa accompanies her."

As the young physician entered the parlor with Mrs. Middleford, the first sight that met his eyes made his heart beat fast. Louisa was seated by a window with some sewing. She put aside the fabric, rose to her feet, and quickly crossed the room to take his hands. He kissed her lightly and briefly on her soft cheek. This was his usual mode of greeting all his female cousins after long absences, but in Louisa's case, as they both well knew, it meant far more than mere familial affection.

"You are looking well, Lou," he remarked, compressing his lips together to keep them from trembling.

"And so are you, Wes," she replied. "Do come and sit down with us. You know we have many questions for you."

He took a seat between the two ladies and began to answer all their inquiries about Harriott and Mary and their husbands.

"They are well," he began. "They are all well. Harriott, well, she is her usual competent self, and busies herself seeing to every need and comfort of her husband, who dotes on her more than ever. Mary is also doing well, and has hinted to me that she and her husband may leave South Carolina."

"To go to England?" Louisa inquired eagerly.

Dr. Frost shrugged.

"I don't know, but that does seem likely."

"Has Major Mitchell fully recovered?" asked Mrs. Middleford.

"I think he has not fully regained his strength and stamina, but he will. He is much better, and was fitted for a wooden leg last week. He'll do well with that."

"It quite broke our hearts to hear of his terrible wound," Mrs. Middleford lamented quietly. "After all the suffering he endured to save his limb from that first wound—"

She paused at the sound of the front door opening. Moments later, Charlotte and Rebecca appeared in the doorway. The younger sister seemed to freeze in place when she saw her cousin, with an expression that wavered between agony and joy.

"What is wrong, dear?" her mother asked anxiously, thinking immediately of her young man.

"Oh, Mama," she sobbed. "Christopher—he has been very

unwell since yesterday. But I have been praying for him, and now I see—my prayers have been answered. Wes! Wes! You can help him!"

Dr. Frost had crossed the room to see about her, and when he took her in his arms, she burst into tears.

"There, dear," he comforted her. "I will certainly help him if I can."

"The other doctor," she said haltingly. "He is so old, and I don't think he knows what to do for him. Reverend Mr. Wilson is looking for another physician, but I know that you are the best of doctors. Will you go with me there now?"

"Of course, Lottie. I have brought my medical bag."

"I'll go with you, too," said Louisa.

* * *

The boy was feverish and weak, and Dr. Frost looked down on his new patient with great concern. He had seen men in this condition many times during the war, and often as not, it only worsened in a steady progression towards death.

Charlotte had taken her usual place beside his bed and was gently wiping a damp, cool cloth across his forehead, while young Wilson gazed at her wistfully with his one good eye. A battle wound had left a large oblique scar just over his left eye and caused and a slight drooping of the eyelid, and there were a number of smaller scars on his face resembling pock marks, from tiny pieces of shell that had struck him. The same blast had taken away the lower part of his left arm.

The boy's father, a slender, handsome man of sixty with silver gray hair, stood by Charlotte, his head lowered in prayer.

"Lottie," said the doctor, "I need to take a look at the injured arm. Have you seen it?"

"Yes," she whispered.

Dr. Frost rolled back the sleeve of the boy's nightshirt and uncovered the stump that remained just below the elbow. The skin had closed and healed in a scarred mass, but there was an angry red streak going up the arm to the shoulder. It began at the line of a red scar a little above the elbow, where there had been a deep laceration. The doctor touched the scar, and his patient cried out in pain.

"I shall have to reopen that wound," he announced. "I suspect there is a fragment of shell beneath it. It is so close to the bone, I think it has pierced it. It must come out, or his blood will be poisoned beyond hope."

Charlotte leaned down and put her face very close to Christopher.

"Will you permit Dr. Frost to perform this operation, dear?" she asked.

"I think I must," he answered hoarsely.

She kissed the boy, and he managed a brief, feeble smile.

Dr. Frost took Christopher's father aside and spoke with him outside the door, and Reverend Wilson soon left the house on an urgent errand. He returned within a quarter of an hour with a small supply of chloroform and carbolic acid. By that time, everything was ready for the operation. Clean towels and bandages had been laid out, and the surgical instruments were arranged on a table beside the bed next to basins of clean water and an oil lamp.

Dr. Frost rolled up his sleeves, but before he took hold of the scalpel, he asked Charlotte to leave the room. She protested.

"I think it best that you are not present, Lottie," he said firmly. "I mustn't have any distractions, you understand."

"I'll be very quiet," she promised. "I shan't faint."

The doctor looked at Louisa, and she put an arm around her younger sister and led her out of the room, closing the door behind them.

"Mr. Wilson," said the doctor, "I shall need your assistance. Can I rely on you to remain calm?"

"For my son's sake," replied the minister, "I could bear anything."

"I shall need you to hold the lamp for me in such a way that I can best see into the incision. To do that, you must look at it, too, for a least a few moments."

"I understand," said Rev. Wilson. "I can do that."

"Very well, then. Let's begin."

After the anesthesia was administered, Dr. Frost propped the boy's injured arm on a small wooden chest, the top of which was padded by a small stack of towels, and he began to make the incision.

Outside the room, Louisa and Charlotte paced arm in arm, then sat down on a sofa in the parlor, exhausted with anticipation and anxiety, though both were praying fervently.

Less than thirty minutes passed, but it seemed to them that hours had gone by when they finally heard the door of the bedroom open. Hurrying in that direction, they met Rev. Wilson in the hall, and saw that his face wore an expression of relief. He was carrying a small bundle of towels wrapped up so as to conceal the bloodied ones.

"Dr. Frost said the operation was a success," he told the girls. "He removed a piece of shell, and believes that Christopher will do much better now."

"Thank God! Thank God!" gasped Charlotte.

"May we go in now?" asked Louisa.

"He says you may."

Though both sisters felt somewhat weak in the knees, they made their way into the bedroom and found the patient sleeping peacefully. Dr. Frost was putting on his coat to cover the blood stains on his sleeves.

"I found what I was looking for," he said. "Lodged in the bone, as I suspected. I found no other fragments in his body. I think he has a good chance of recovery now."

Charlotte rushed over and embraced her cousin.

"Oh, Wes!" she cried. "I knew you were a godsend! I knew it! Oh, I am so grateful to you, cousin. Thank you!"

Louisa, who had been gazing at him admiringly, also added her thanks.

"Mama told us it was providential that you came to Columbia at this time," she said. "And I see she is right about that."

"I'm very glad that I could be of some help to this young man."

Weston was looking at Louisa as he spoke, and thought he saw in her eyes, for the first time, a light he had been waiting and hoping to see for many years.

The following day, when they all returned to the Wilson residence, Dr. Frost's patient was looking and feeling better. His fever had abated, and he had regained some appetite. After his examination, Charlotte sat with him and lovingly spooned sips of chicken broth into his mouth.

Rev. Wilson thanked Dr. Frost again profusely, and tried to offer him payment for his services, but he flatly refused.

"I did this for Lottie as much for him," he explained. "Besides, once she and your son are married, he and I will be cousins, and I could not take payment to treat a kinsman."

* * *

That evening, Weston sat out on the piazza with Louisa and her sisters. The night was very quiet except for the songs of crickets, and after an hour's conversation, the girls fell strangely silent. There was then an exchange of meaning looks among the sisters, and soon, the two youngest rose to their feet and strolled off arm in arm to the farthest end of the piazza.

Louisa looked at Weston with an air of expectancy. When she spoke, he thought for a moment that he must be dreaming.

"Is there something you wish to ask me, Wes?"

"Can it be true?" he thought, suddenly gripped with such emotion that he almost felt faint.

"Will you—will you marry me, Lou?" he heard himself saying in a faltering voice.

She smiled and answered, "I will marry you, Wes."

Trembling a little, he went to his knees before her and took her hands in his.

"I should have done this before I asked," he laughed nervously.

Louisa laughed, too, and agreed.

"Dear Louisa," he said tenderly. "I shall do all that is in my power to take care of you and make you happy. It is all I have ever wanted of life."

"I love you, Wes," she responded warmly.

Louisa and Weston drew closer until their lips met, but their first lovers' kiss was interrupted by shrieks and cries of celebration from Charlotte and Rebecca, who rushed over to the couple to offer their congratulations.

CHAPTER FIFTEEN

One afternoon Harriott walked into her husband's room expecting to find him in his chair reading, as he usually did this time of day, but the chair was empty, and his book was set aside on a table, next to a letter from Captain Wyatt he had received that morning. She found James in the room next to the study. Balanced on his crutches, he stood facing the two paintings he had created some four and a half years past. She came to his side and saw that his expression was gloomy.

"I am very proud of your work," she said, trying to brighten his mood. "It is really masterful. I hardly knew I had married such a fine artist."

James sighed and lowered his eyes.

"I was so inspired when I painted them," he said in a quiet, pensive tone. "So inspired, and so hopeful. There is no hope now."

In the silence that followed he turned to Harriott and studied her face with eyes full of a mysterious hesitancy. She could see that something very important was on his mind.

"Have you heard from Mary lately?" he asked.

"Not lately, no. Is there some news in Henry's letter?"

"He is taking her back to England with him, as soon as they

can obtain passage," James informed her somberly.

"Mary is such a dear friend. I shall miss her terribly," Harriott lamented. "But I am not surprised."

"I'm glad for them," he said. "There is nothing left for him here now, and she will be better off in England, at least materially."

Harriott's head was lowered, and she stared down at the carpet in sad reflection. When James spoke again, she looked up abruptly.

"Shall we go to England?" he wondered aloud, to her great surprise.

"Are you serious?" she asked.

"Would you consider it?"

His look and tone were very much in earnest.

"You are serious!" she marveled.

"I am."

"What—what about your mother?"

"She is welcome to come with us if she wishes to, but I doubt she will leave South Carolina."

"How long have you been thinking of this? Was it—Henry's letter?"

"No, I've been contemplating this idea for a while—for weeks. I wanted to be sure about it in my own mind before I broached the subject with you. Now I am sure."

Harriott was speechless for a while, too stunned to think.

"I have some money in England," he went on. "Not a fortune, but enough to live on for a while, for several years if necessary. While I was in Charleston I got out some shipments of cotton to Nassau, and from there to England. I have a cousin in Liverpool who has kept the funds safe for me. He married an English lady from a very fine family, and was blockade running—"

James stopped when he saw that there were tears in

Harriott's eyes, and suddenly, he looked on the verge of tears himself.

"You think badly of me for wishing to leave? You think it dishonorable?"

"No!" she gasped. "It's that I—I did not know how great your despair was, until now, and it gives me great sorrow."

"It is not despair! It is not!" he groaned with shuddering breaths. "What else can I do? My country—"

He stopped again, suppressing a sob, and she saw him swaying a little on his crutches.

"Please sit down, dear," she urged him, taking his arm.

James carefully lowered himself down to a cushion on the sofa, and Harriott took a seat beside him. He drew in a deep breath and composed himself.

"If circumstances were different for me," he said, "if I were a public man, a person of influence, or means, or had any livelihood or wealth left to me, I would stay and try to…try to salvage what is left of this shipwreck. Someday, when and if I have the means, and am strong again, it would be my duty to return to my state and do what I can for her, and I would, but for now, I think it best for us to go abroad. I know it is asking a great deal of you, Harriott, but I want you to consider it. Will you do that for me?"

After a silence she replied, "Give me time to think it over. I must have a little time."

"May we speak of it again tomorrow?" he asked.

"Yes, tomorrow."

* * *

For the rest of the day, Harriott was preoccupied thinking of the momentous change that could be taking place in her life soon, and the more the picture of such a change was fully realized in her mind, the more she was afraid of it. The idea of leaving her family, her home—all that she knew and loved—filled her with dread.

That night, she was unable to sleep, and after a few restless hours in bed, her husband reached over and touched her face.

"Did I wake you, dear?" she asked apologetically.

"It's all right. I wasn't really sleeping either," he answered softly. "Troubled thoughts keeping you awake?"

His hand was still cradling her face, and he felt her nod.

"I don't want you to be troubled, or fearful, Harriott," said James. "I only want your happiness. That is partly why I think it best for us to go."

His gentle, measured tone gave her the courage to ask, "Dear, have you considered all that this means for us?"

"I have. You mustn't think that under any other circumstances less dire, I would uproot you, take you away from your home and family and friends...but Harriott, our world here is at an end."

"Perhaps...perhaps you are too discouraged just now, too pessimistic," she suggested.

"No, I am quite realistic. In business, I am without a doubt ruined. As an artist, it isn't likely that I could make a living in this state, as nearly everyone else has also been ruined. So I shall be without the means to provide for you. In England, however, there is at least some hope that I could earn money by my painting, and even the possibility of employment in my cousin's company in Liverpool."

Harriott was quiet for a while, and as she pondered everything that he had said, she had to acknowledge that it was all true and reasonable, yet she still recoiled at the thought of leaving her home. A wave of fear passed over her again, and she began to cry.

"I know it will be difficult for you, Harriott," said James. "I feel the tears on your cheek. I know you are afraid…but remember? You were afraid to marry me. Do you regret it?"

"No!"

"Then don't let fear have its way with you in this, either," he said, stroking her hair.

The warmth and assurance of his voice and touch calmed her, and she began to realize that all this time, in the grip of paralyzing anxiety, she had only been thinking of herself. Seeing clearly now how important and necessary this venture was for him, and how much he needed her, she reproached herself for selfishness and weakness. Crushing down her fears, she came to a decision.

"We will go to England," she said tearfully, but firmly. "I have an aunt in New York, and I shall write to her for assistance in obtaining passage for us on a steamer."

With a long exhalation of relief, James pulled her close. Enfolding her in his arms, he whispered a question in her ear.

"Do you remember that house we dreamed of building in Flat Rock?"

"Our English cottage," she said, wiping her eyes.

"Can you not imagine us in a real English cottage now? I could paint, and you could write."

A faint smile lifted the corners of her lips, and she blinked away the last of the tears.

"We'll have that garden, too," he added, smiling. "I promised you all these things, Harriott, and you shall have them."

* * *

That night, when Harriott finally fell asleep beside her husband, she had a dream. It was unlike any other dream she had ever experienced; there was an unmistakable significance to it; it did away with much of her fear and left her confident as she woke up the next morning, that she had made the right decision.

In this dream, she and James traveled up the coast on a steamer to New York, where she saw and spoke with her elderly, wealthy aunt. The lady embraced her and told her that she need not fear, promising an inheritance. The next thing Harriott knew, with inexplicable, dreamlike swiftness, she and her husband were aboard a large steam vessel, standing together on the deck hand in hand, and as the dream ended, the ship was underway, beginning its long journey to the Old World, and leaving the ruins of their own behind them.

The End

About the Author

Karen Stokes, an archivist with the South Carolina Historical Society in Charleston, S.C., is the co-editor of *Faith, Valor, and Devotion: The Civil War Letters of William Porcher DuBose*, published by the University of South Carolina Press in 2010. She is also the author of another non-fiction book, *South Carolina Civilians in Sherman's Path*, released in June 2012 by The History Press.

Belles, inspired by South Carolinians' Civil War letters found in the SCHS archives, is her first venture into historical fiction.

Other Titles by the Author

FICTION:

The Immortals: A Story of Love and War

Honor in the Dust

The Soldier's Ghost: A Tale of Charleston

Belles: A Carolina Love Story

NON-FICTION:

Carolina Love Letters

(Co-editor) *Days of Destruction: Augustine Thomas Smythe and the Civil War Siege of Charleston*

A Legion of Devils: Sherman in South Carolina

Confederate South Carolina: True Stories of Civilians, Soldiers and the War

The Immortal 600: Surviving Civil War Charleston and Savannah

(Co-editor) *A Confederate Englishman: The Civil War Letters of Henry Wemyss Feilden*

South Carolina Civilians in Sherman's Path

(Co-editor) *Faith, Valor, and Devotion: The Civil War Correspondence of William Porcher DuBose*

SOUTHERN LITERATURE is the glory of American culture. Faulkner, O'Connor, Warren, Lytle, Davidson, Gordon, Percy, Chappell, Berry will be known as long as Western civilization survives and long after today's politicians, "experts," and celebrity writers are forgotten. Another of the greats, George Garrett, wrote that "all signs indicate that Southern literature, far from being on its last legs and far from representing a falling off from earlier and better days, seems very much alive." Shotwell Publishing has supported Garrett's witness by launching GREEN ALTAR BOOKS—a collection of Southern fiction and poetry.

For more information on this and other SOUTHERN titles, Please visit us at ShotwellPublishing.com.

Available from Shotwell Publishing

GREEN ALTAR BOOKS (Literary Imprint)

A New England Romance & Other SOUTHERN Stories by Randall Ivey

Belles: A Carolina Love Story by Karen Stokes

Honor in the Dust by Karen Stokes

The Immortals: A Story of Love and War by Karen Stokes

The Soldier's Ghost: A Tale of Charleston by Karen Stokes

Tiller (Clay Bank County Series) by James Everett Kibler

GOLD-BUG (Mystery & Suspense Imprint)

Billy Jo by Michael Andrew Grissom

To Jekyll and Hide by Martin L. Wilson

Splintered: A New Orleans Tale by Brandi Perry

NONFICTION TITLES

A Legion of Devils: Sherman in South Carolina by Karen Stokes

Annals of the Stupid Party: Republicans Before Trump (The Wilson Files) by Clyde N. Wilson

Carolina Love Letters by Karen Stokes

Confederaphobia: An American Epidemic by Paul C. Graham

The Devil's Town: Hot Springs During the Gangster Era by Philip Leigh

Dismantling the Republic by Jerry C. Brewer

Dixie Rising: Rules for Rebels by James R. Kennedy

Emancipation Hell: The Tragedy Wrought By Lincoln's Emancipation Proclamation by Kirkpatrick Sale

Lies My Teacher Told Me: The True History of the War for Southern Independence by Clyde N. Wilson

Maryland, My Maryland: The Cultural Cleansing of a Small Southern State by Joyce Bennett.

My Own Darling Wife: Letters from a Confederaate Volunteer. Edited with introduction by Andrew P. Calhoun

Nullification: Reclaiming Consent of the Governed (The Wilson Files) by Clyde N. Wilson

The Old South: 50 Essential Books (Sothern Reader's Guide) by Clyde N. Wilson

Punished with Poverty: The Suffering South by James R. & Walter D. Kennedy

Segregation: Federal Policy or Racism? by John Chodes

Southern Independence. Why War? by Dr. Charles T. Pace

Southerner, Take Your Stand! by John Vinson

Washington's KKK: The Union League During Southern Reconstruction by John Chodes.

When the Yankees Come: Former South Carolina Slaves Remember Sherman's Invasion. Edited with introduction by Paul C. Graham

The Yankee Problem: An American Dilemma (The Wison Files) by Clyde N. Wilson

Free Book Offer

Sign-up for new release notification and receive a FREE DOWNLOADABLE EDITION of *Lies My Teacher Told Me: The True History of the War for Southern Independence* by Dr. Clyde N. Wilson by visiting FreeLiesBook.com or by texting the word "Dixie" to 345345. You can always unsubscribe and keep the book, so you've got nothing to lose!

Southern Without Apology.